Alexis's
half-baked
idea

This book is a work of fiction. Any references to historical events, real people, or real places are used fictitiously. Other names, characters, places, and events are products of the author's imagination, and any resemblance to actual events or places or persons, living or dead, is entirely coincidental.

SIMON SPOTLIGHT
An imprint of Simon & Schuster Children's Publishing Division
1230 Avenue of the Americas, New York, New York 10020
First Simon Spotlight paperback edition June 2019
Copyright © 2019 by Simon & Schuster, Inc.
All rights reserved, including the right of reproduction
in whole or in part in any form.
SIMON SPOTLIGHT and colophon are registered trademarks of
Simon & Schuster, Inc.
Text by Elizabeth Doyle Carey
Chapter header illustrations by Daniel Tornow
Designed by Laura Roode
For information about special discounts for bulk purchases, please contact
Simon & Schuster Special Sales at 1-866-506-1949 or
business@simonandschuster.com.
Manufactured in the United States of America 0519 OFF
2 4 6 8 10 9 7 5 3 1
ISBN 978-1-5344-4067-8 (hc)
ISBN 978-1-5344-4066-1 (pbk)
ISBN 978-1-5344-4068-5 (eBook)
Library of Congress Catalog Card Number 2019932880

CUPCAKE DIARIES

Alexis's half-baked idea

by coco simon

Simon Spotlight

New York   London   Toronto   Sydney   New Delhi

CHAPTER 1

Party Planning

$\mathcal{N}$o one can drive you as crazy as your sister can—that's what I always say. Sisters are forever— that's what my mom always says. Does this mean my sister will be driving me crazy forever?

None of my best friends has a sister. Katie is an only child. But Katie's mom is engaged, so she sort of has a stepsister now. Mia *was* an only child, but when her mom got remarried, she gained a stepbrother. And Emma has three brothers (one of whom is my crush, Matt). So whenever I complain about my older sister, Dylan, my friends all shush me and say how lucky I am to *have* a sister, and one so *talented* and *cool* and *stylish* and . . .YUCK! Sometimes I think they like her better than they like me.

For example, it's my birthday tomorrow. *My* birthday, not Dylan's. And my friends decided to plan a party for me, which is supersweet. Only they got Dylan to help them, and then they let her take over, like she always does, and now they're all "Dylan thinks . . ." and "Dylan loves . . ." and "Dylan said . . ." But what about me, Alexis? What do I think and love and say? *Hmmm?*

What's even more annoying is that my friends have been spending more time with Dylan, working on my party, than they have with me. I've actually texted them to do stuff, and they've said no, they have plans. And the plans are with Dylan, to "work" on the party. But sometimes I think there's more fun than work going on. I mean, how long can it take to make a playlist and choose a paper tablecloth? I've tried chiming in when I can, but they just shush me and say everything's going to be a "big, juicy, beautiful surprise," which is a Dylan-sounding phrase if ever I've heard one. (She talks like a game show host a lot.)

They even booted me from our weekly Cupcake Club meeting because they had to plan the cupcakes for my party. (We usually baked cupcakes for one of our favorite and longstanding clients, Mona, on Fridays.) They had Dylan go instead of me, saying she would "represent the Beckers." Do they seriously think Dylan knows more about cupcakes than I do? I bet she's just going to blow the party budget on the cupcakes. She's that carefree type who'd add gold sprinkles *and* molten marshmallows to a recipe, with total disregard for the cost. I shudder to think of it.

I was frustrated, too, because Dylan has always made it perfectly clear that she has no interest in my "nerdy little Cupcake Club." But now that she needs my friends' help with the party and the cupcakes, the Cupcake Club is just fine with her. Wait, I have to stop here and talk about my party.

Here's what I know so far: It's going to be held here, at my house. There will be cupcakes, of course, and music. I know that at least my three besties will be there, and Dylan, of course. I don't know who else is coming except . . . my crush (and Emma's big brother) Matt Taylor! I only know he's coming because he blurted it out to me two weeks ago when I was over at their house for a Friday cupcake meeting. He mentioned that he hoped I'd be serving his favorite cupcake flavor (bacon and salted caramel, of course) at my party, and my face turned five shades of pink while Emma chewed him out for revealing party details.

The truth is, besides my besties, he is the only guest I really care about. I know he's not my boyfriend—I'm too young for a boyfriend, according to my mom, which is actually kind of fine—but it's superfun to like him and chat with him and joke around when we see each other. He's very cute—tall and sporty with blond hair and twinkly blue eyes—and he's goal-minded, just like me. He is very involved in sports at school and with his travel teams, and he runs an independent graphic design business on the side, making flyers and posters and stuff for kids and even adult clients. One of the things I really like about him is that we can talk business and really learn from each other and get excited about things other people might not understand, like BOGOs (Buy One, Get One promotions) and CTAs (those are Calls to Action, or what you want your ads to inspire people to do). We geek out on that stuff together, and it's cool.

Anyway, I am pretty sure he has a crush on me as well. He has given me a hug a couple of times and a kiss on the cheek, and we have danced at parties and exchanged Valentines. I mean, it's nothing formal and we're not a couple, but we know each other pretty well now, and we enjoy each other's company a lot. So as long as he's at the party, along with my besties, that's all that matters.

Actually, even though I'm eager to see what Dylan and my friends came up with for my party, my excitement is almost more from a business standpoint. Like, I'm not a real fun party person. I'm all about budget and how to stretch a dollar. I always want to see what people can accomplish within certain restrictions. A big, splashy party filled with random acquaintances isn't really my idea of a good time. It is *Dylan's* idea of a good time, though. I'd rather just chill with my close friends, since, unlike Dylan, I'm not the popular type.

I sighed, hearing peals of laughter coming from the party committee meeting (aka Cupcake Club meeting) downstairs. Well, I'd just have to harness this time to get ahead on my work so I could fully enjoy the day tomorrow, since the party would eat into my usual homework slot.

Plopping down on my desk chair, I opened the heavy black cover of my planner to see what was due Monday and also what my long-term projects were for school and for a club I belonged to, the Future Business Leaders of America. Nothing too bad right now, which was good and bad. I do love diving into a meaty project on the weekend, but at the same time I was feeling a little scattered due to my party. So maybe it was better that there was nothing that required a lot of concentration right now! Next, I scanned our Cupcake Club to-do list to see if I owed proposals to anyone or if I needed to pay any invoices or send bills to clients, but we were in good shape, pretty much thanks to me. Failing to plan is planning to fail—that's what I always say. I sighed. What else could I organize since I had this window of free time now?

I swiveled my desk chair around and looked at my room. Bed made, desk organized, clothes put away neatly, e-mails all answered . . . Hmm. I thought about my upcoming schedule and decided I'd plan my outfit for the party, right now! That was a good use of my free time.

I went over to my closet and started flipping through the hangers. It wasn't like I didn't know what was in there. I don't like fashion, but I am a stern editor of my clothes. If something doesn't work, it is out, out, *out*. First, I offer it to Dylan (she never wants anything of mine); next, I offer it to my friends (Katie sometimes takes stuff; Emma and Mia never do). And if no one close to me wants it, I put it in the donation bag that my mom keeps by our back door. Right now, I didn't have a ton of dressy clothes, since I am not a superdressy person.

I like to look nice, so I won't wear ripped jeans or anything, but I am not a girlie-girl dressy person. I have some plain skirts and pants and one or two dressy tops I could add in order to jazz them up. That is really my style. Also, I hate to shop. Spending money puts me in a bad mood, and unlike Dylan, I hate trying stuff on.

I pulled out a pair of black twill leggings ("jeggings," Dylan called them when she handed them down to me), a denim miniskirt, and two different tops, and I laid them out on my bed.

One of the tops was pink cotton, sleeveless, and ruffly at the neck. The other top was a sparkly green polka-dotted sweater that my granny gave me for Christmas. I swapped them around so the pink top was over the miniskirt instead of the jeggings.

"There we go!" I smiled. The green sweater and black jeggings were a match: cute *and* practical. That was easy! I put the pink top and the skirt away, neatly spacing the hangers in the closet for maximum airflow and ease of use, then I hung the party outfit on a hook on the inside of my closet door so it would be ready to go tomorrow.

What now? I went back to my desk. Maybe I'd quiz myself for the Spanish test scheduled for next Friday. Yes, it was a week away, but those flash cards weren't going to study themselves! Suddenly, there was a ruckus in the hall, and my friends came bursting into my room all at once, squealing.

"Ooooh, Lexi! Tomorrow's going to be so fun!" said Emma, flinging herself onto my bed. I winced as the neatly made covers scrunched and bunched under her.

Mia sank gracefully to the floor. "We have our work cut out for us in the morning. Not that it's going to be work!" she added hurriedly. "We'd do anything for you, Alexis. Plus, Dylan makes it all so fun. . . ."

Katie agreed. "Maybe we should add her to the Cupcake Club as sort of our party planning services person?"

"Aaargh! Enough!" I cried, clapping my hands once, so hard they stung. Everyone looked at me in surprise.

"What's up, Lex?" asked Emma, bewildered.

My face burned with embarrassment. "I . . . I don't know how to say this without sounding awful, but . . ."

Katie caught on immediately; she's the most thoughtful and sensitive of us all. She hopped up and came and put her arm around me. "I get it. You don't have to say anything. We're sorry."

Emma and Mia still looked confused.

I sighed heavily. I was not happy.

"What is it?" asked Mia.

Katie patted my back. "Alexis feels a little left out and"—she glanced at me to see if she was on the right track, and I nodded—"a little bit tired of hearing about Dylan. Am I right?"

I closed my eyes in shame and nodded again. "It's not that I don't love her and that I'm not grateful . . . ," I began in a whisper.

Emma smacked her forehead. "Duh! I'm so sorry. We've just been having so much fun with her. I'd forgotten how cool—"

"Shush!" scolded Katie. "This is Alexis's birthday party, and we are excited to celebrate *Alexis* tomorrow. Now, Alexis, we came to get you so we could do some of the baking for Mona tomorrow, and then the rest of us are going to move over to my house and make the party cupcakes for tomorrow."

"Which are top secret!" cried Mia.

"But you're gonna love them!" added Emma.

"So let's head on down and do what we do best, okay, girls?" Katie finished.

I am not superhuggy, but I reached over and gave Katie a squeeze with my arm looped around her shoulders.

"Thanks, pal," I whispered, and she squeezed back.

Downstairs, Dylan was nowhere to be seen, thankfully. The four of us Cupcakers fell into our weekly rhythm of preheating, measuring, stirring, and more as we baked for our main client, Mona, who owned The Special Day bridal shop. Other than the fact that the measuring cups at my house stink (they're all dented and old so they're not very accurate), we were jamming along. I love it when we're in our groove—it makes me so happy that we are a well-oiled machine—and we chat easily about work and life while we bake. This week, Emma was telling us her plans for the upcoming school talent show. She's an amazing flute player and was trying to decide if she'd play a difficult solo piece she's been practicing for weeks or an easier duet with her teacher on the piano. I, of course, wanted to know if there will be refreshments at the talent show, and if so, who I can contact to see if they'd like to order some cupcakes!

"I'll find out," offered Emma. "Then I'll put you in touch."

While we were discussing the talent show, my mom came home from work.

"Hi, girlie-os!" she said cheerfully, albeit a little

distracted. She lowered her briefcase to the kitchen floor while reading something on her phone.

"Hi, Mrs. Becker!" my friends called.

"Oh, too bad!" said my mom, reacting to whatever she just read. She looked up and found my eyes. "Granny and Granddad won't be able to make it to your party tomorrow after all. They send you all their love, but they couldn't make their timetable work if they set out in this direction first."

"Oh, that's okay," I said. "We did *just* see them and say good-bye to them." My dad's parents had been working toward their life's dream over the past year. They'd sold their house and gotten rid of most of their possessions. Tomorrow, the movers will put the rest of their stuff in storage, and then my grandparents will be hitting the road in a tricked-out RV to tour the United States, visiting their children, grandchildren, and old friends all across the country. We went to a big going-away party for them last weekend, and they were so excited. It was cute.

"Granny said they send you their happiest birthday wishes, plus a big squeeze," added my mom, smiling at me.

I smiled back. "Thanks."

We finished making Mona's cupcakes (my favorite: vanilla mini cupcakes with vanilla frosting, as usual, because everything in her shop is white!), and my friends got ready to go to Katie's for baking session number two. I felt a little left out, but suddenly, Dylan appeared on the scene and swooped me upstairs for some pre-party beauty treatments: a hair mask and face mask. It was perfect timing—it made me a tiny bit less sad to see my friends all leave together, and also a little less annoyed with Dylan for the moment. Even though, as they left, my friends sighed and said, "Oh, Dylan. You're the best big sister a girl could ever have!" and other stuff like that.

I just did what my mom always tells me to do when little things are bothering me: I acted like a duck and let it roll off my back.

Quack!

CHAPTER 2

Pre-Party Prep

The day of my party was beautiful, and my dad and I rolled down all the car windows as we drove to drop off Mona's mini cupcakes. My hair billowed in the breeze, and I closed my eyes in the sunshine and felt like a movie star driving along the seashore in California. Except with her dad, but whatever. It was a fun fantasy anyway.

After the mall, he took me straight to my favorite bakery, and we bought sticky caramel cinnamon buns. My dad has a major sweet tooth, but my mom is a health nut, so he's always looking for any excuse (and any partner in crime) to go find some sugar. Today he pulled a birthday candle and a pack of matches out of his pocket and sang happy birthday to me at our table at the bakery. I was embarrassed because everyone in the store chimed in. My dad lives for that kind of silly celebration. It's mortifying while it's going on, but afterward, it's always special and memorable. He's just a guy who likes to enjoy life.

"Happy birthday, sweetheart. Your mother and I are so proud of you. You're a wonderful young lady," said my dad, beaming at me.

"Thanks, Dad. You're a wonderful young man, and I'm proud of you too," I teased him, and giggled as I took a bite of my amazing birthday bun.

"Wasn't it nice of Dylan to plan this party for you?" he asked, tucking into his cinnamon treat.

"Umm-hmm," I agreed through a mouthful of dough.

"She's very thoughtful that way," he said, shaking his head in admiration. "No detail is too small."

"Mmmm," I agreed again.

"I remember when you were born, she wanted to be your mom. She kept trying to take you out of your bassinet and put you in the stroller to push you around. She was a little kid herself! We had to put a lock on your bedroom door, up high, where she couldn't reach it."

"Umm." I'd heard this before, so I had nothing to add.

"She's always been so good to you . . ," he said wistfully.

Somehow my cinnamon bun had become lodged in my throat. I gulped some milk and swallowed hard. "Right," I said, hoping he was finished.

"You know, Dylan's . . ."

I put my fist down on the table, a little harder than I'd meant to (I think). It made a pretty loud thump. My dad looked up at me questioningly.

"It's my birthday, Dad. I know Dylan's great and all, but does everything always have to be about her?"

My dad's eyebrows shot up and his mouth dropped open in surprise. "What? No! It's not all about Dylan. I'm sorry. I just was thinking back to those days, when you were newly born." He shook his head as if to clear it. "I didn't mean it that way."

I waved my hand to clear the air. "It's fine," I said briskly. "Don't worry about it. Let's change the subject."

"Okay . . . so . . . who's coming to the party later?" he asked, forking another gooey hunk of bun into his mouth.

I mentioned the obvious: the Cupcakers, Matt Taylor, maybe one or two other kids from school, and then I shrugged. "I don't really know. I'm happy with anyone and anything. I don't really have any strong preferences. Just that it not be over-the-top and wasteful."

"That's my girl," he said, smiling.

We chatted about school, and then we finished up and headed home. I'd had a nice time, of course, but the Dylan thing still stuck in my throat a little.

That afternoon, Dylan appeared in my doorway, one hand on her hip and one on the doorframe. "Ready for your primping, party girl?" she asked, batting her eyelashes at me.

I was doing my Spanish flash cards and happy for the distraction. "Okay. We still have almost two hours, though," I said, looking at my watch.

Dylan sighed. "Lexi, Lexi, Lexi. Will you ever learn? Beauty takes time! It takes patience! It takes strength and fortitude. You don't think I just wake up looking like this, do you?"

I rolled my eyes. The thing was, she was only half joking. "Fine. So, what first?"

"Shower. Shampoo twice and then condition. Then we'll do hair and makeup. Don't forget to shave your legs," she ordered as she turned and marched away.

"I'm wearing pants!" I cried.

"Not for sure, you're not!" she called over her shoulder.

Rolling my eyes again, I headed in to shower.

Dylan blew my hair out so it was pin straight and smooth. Then she put it in big fat rollers to create "volume" and "lift." She had me put on my outfit, shaking her head in dismay at the jeggings and green sweater.

"You're not showing any leg?" she asked, scoping me up and down with a critical eye.

"Dylan! It's a party at home, in our living room!" I protested. "We're not going to a club!"

"What*ever*! It's your party!" she said. "I was just thinking with your boyfriend coming and all. . . ."

"He's not my boyfriend!" I cried.

"*Yet,*" Dylan said firmly. "Now sit and let me do your makeup."

"I don't want too much. Mom will make me come back up and take it off, and I hate that. It makes my eyes all sting-y and red."

Dylan scoffed. "Don't you think I know the limitations we must suffer under around here? We're doing clear mascara, a hint of brown eyeliner, and pink lip gloss. That's all." She sighed as she pushed me down into the chair at her dressing table and studied me critically.

"Would you let me pluck your eyebrows?"

"What? No way! That would hurt!"

"Beauty is pain, but it's probably too late anyway. We don't want any redness or swelling this close to the party," she said, assessing her cosmetics choices.

Redness? Swelling? No, thanks!

Dylan spun me around on the chair and set to work.

Fifteen minutes later she said, "Voilà! My work here is done!" and spun me back around to look.

I didn't look too different to the naked eye, but I could see everything was a tiny bit enhanced. I did look good, I had to admit.

"Thanks, Dilly. I like it," I said. I smiled at her in the mirror.

She smiled back, pleased with her handiwork. "Leave the hair till the last minute, and we'll take it down right before everyone arrives. Now scram so I can get ready!"

I passed my mom in the hallway, and she said. "Wow—you look great! Dylan did a wonderful job on your makeup!"

Grrr! Can Dylan do no wrong?

I started down the stairs and saw Katie bustle

past. She and the other Cupcakers had come early to get everything ready for the party. She spotted me and scolded, "Back upstairs! Wait for us to come get you!"

Hmm. I turned and went back to my room. I didn't really have anything to do. I sat in my desk chair and spun lazily, first in one direction, then in the other. I wondered how the party would go and if I'd like it. Who else was coming? What had my friends brought to decorate the living room? Maybe some flowers? What kind of music would we dance to? There would certainly be snacks. I know there were definitely going to be cupcakes, but what sort? They couldn't give *everyone* plain vanilla mini cupcakes.

I sighed, restless and kind of nervous. What if I didn't like the party? What if I didn't think it was fun? Could I fake having a good time? Would anyone be able to tell?

To kill some time and distract myself, I turned on my computer and went to my favorite websites, where I sometimes go to relax: I was just too nervous to focus on my studies. So I checked out some stationery and office-supply websites. I love how everything on those sites is so organized and neat, ready for people to get to work or just relax. It's so inspiring. Right as I was studying a sale on folders, there was thudding on the stairs, and my friends bounded into my room to change.

"Lex, you're gonna love it! It looks ah-*mazing* down there!" said Emma, whipping off her clothes. Ever since she became a model, Emma has no shyness at all about changing in front of us. She says she's gotten used to everyone poking and prodding her, and she can't be too self-conscious. Meanwhile, Katie ducked into the bathroom to change, and Mia was in my closet.

"Don't give away any secrets, Em!" Mia called out in a muffled voice.

"I'm not!" protested Emma. "You're going to like it, though," she whispered. "It looks great."

I was feeling excited now.

Ten minutes later, the gang was ready.

"Okay, Lex, now we're going to blindfold you and lead you downstairs," said Mia.

"Blindfold? Seriously?" I laughed.

"It was Dylan's idea," said Emma. "She's waiting downstairs already. She wants to be the one to take off the blindfold when you get there."

I raised an eyebrow at Katie, but she just shrugged. "Go for it?" she said, but it was more like a request than a question.

I sighed and turned to let Emma wrap one of Dylan's gauzy scarves around my head. Then I let them lead me out of my room, down the hall and stairs, and into the living room.

As if on cue they all started singing happy birthday, and I heard Dylan whisper close to my ear, "Happy Birthday, Lexi!" and the scarf fell away.

I opened my eyes and gasped! I couldn't believe what I saw.

CHAPTER 3

Cakefetti!

All the living room furniture had been pushed to the walls, opening up the center of the room, upon which had been laid a plastic dance floor with a hot-pink–and-orange checkerboard pattern. The ceiling of the room was entirely filled with colorful paper lanterns with little illumination sticks inside them, giving the room a soft glow. Each of the lanterns had short ribbons hanging down from them, and a dangling little hot pink cardboard *A*. The shades were pulled down, and the window frames were outlined in LED strips that pulsed in different colors, and suspended from the ceiling in the middle of the room was a disco ball slowly spinning and reflecting twinkling light all over. Through the doorway to the dining room, I spied a table loaded with drinks and snacks, including platters of cup-cakes, some of which appeared to be red velvet, my new favorite.

"Say something!" said Mia, laughing as she made a little heart with her hands.

I realized my jaw was hanging open, and I closed it and blinked back sudden tears. "I . . . I can't believe you guys did all this . . . for me!"

"It's because we love you!" cried Emma, grabbing me in a hug and dancing me around the room.

"It's incredible!" I called over my shoulder to the others. "I love it! Thank you all so much!"

Dylan was beaming, and she clapped her hands and then clasped them in front of her chest while she watched me. "I'm just excited about the play-list!" she exclaimed. "I know how much you love to dance, so we gave it our all!"

"Come see the food!" urged Katie, and she grabbed me by the arm and dragged me through to the dining room. "Your mom let us break all the Becker dietary restrictions. There are mini que-sadillas with seven-layer dip, and pigs in a blanket, and these tiny pizza bites, plus chips and guaca-mole. There are three kinds of cupcakes—vanilla; red velvet, since that's your new favorite; and salted caramel and bacon, for you-know-who, and—look! We have a toppings bar, so people can put whatever toppings they want on the cupcakes! There's crushed Oreo cookies, and chopped Rice Krispies treats, and candy corn, and Red Hots, crumbled bacon, and M&M's. . . . And over here we have the drinks. There's Arnold Palmer, and hibiscus iced tea, and fruit punch with Sprite. . . ."

I couldn't believe it. Someone had even made note of the fact that red velvet was my new favorite cupcake flavor. I think I had mentioned it only once, two or three weeks ago! I kept shaking my head in wonder. "This is so much work! And so expensive and over-the-top! I can't believe you did all this!"

"Dylan really knows how to throw a party!" said Mia. Then she clapped her hand over her mouth and laughed. "Sorry," she whispered.

"No, you're right. She really does." I turned and went into the living room to look for Dylan, who was tweaking some of the lanterns in the living room. Quickly, I crossed over and said, "Dilly . . . thanks a milly!" We both laughed as we hugged. "I love this party. It's amazing!" I said into her shoulder, and right then, the doorbell rang and the party officially started.

❁

About twenty-five kids arrived over the course of the next hour. Matt didn't arrive in the first hour, but I knew not to expect him early—Emma said he had two games today and would be rushing to make it to the party in between. That made me feel good. Of the kids who came, they were mostly school friends: classmates and associates from the Future Business Leaders of America—all kids I wouldn't necessarily hang out with outside of school but who were perfectly nice—and a smattering of Dylan's friends. Having high schoolers there jazzed up the party and made it feel cooler, which I liked. I'm not much of a small talker—I leave that kind of stuff to Dylan—so I stayed on the dance floor and showed off some of the moves I've picked up from my favorite show, *Celebrity Ballroom*.

I danced a lot and sang until my voice was hoarse. In the middle of one song, about halfway through the party, I spied Matt in the doorway, his hair wet and his cheeks pink, as if he had rushed over. My heart leaped with excitement as my stomach dropped in nervousness. *Eek! Matt Taylor is at my birthday party,* every cell in my body sang out. Emma danced over and nudged me, making sure I had seen him. I couldn't keep the stupid grin off my face, even as I tried to twirl around her to block Matt from seeing we were noticing him. It wouldn't be good to look too eager. I didn't want to go over there yet. I thought maybe I should let Matt come to me. Emma danced away, and I found myself with my FBLA pals, in a conga line headed up by my friend Nikil.

The next time I looked back at Matt, Dylan was chatting with him, and they were laughing. Oh no! The Taylors were family friends of ours, so Matt and Dylan have spent time together over the years. He'd even been invited to Dylan's upcoming birthday party. I wasn't worried about awkwardness—just the opposite. If I knew Dylan, she was talking me up right now, telling some embellished story to make me look like a romantic heroine. "Oh, Matt, did I ever tell you about the time Alexis had to dive into a shark tank at the aquarium to save a baby?" Even worse, it wouldn't be out of character for her to end the story by saying "And that's why you need to marry Alexis!"

Dylan has to be stopped!

Frantically, I glanced around to see if one of the Cupcakers was available to interrupt Dylan's advertising speech before she went too far. I finally caught Emma's eye and waved to Dylan and Matt, making urgent throat-cutting gestures while trying to be subtle. Emma, bless her heart, saw what was going on and bolted to the dining room. She knew Dylan too well.

I scurried to catch up with the conga line as it snaked through the front hall and around to the kitchen. I realized we were going to end up going through the dining room, and I decided I couldn't prolong my avoidance of saying hi to Matt. He'd notice. As we sashayed around the kitchen island (and my mom giggled from her perch at the kitchen table), I took a deep breath and steeled my nerves. I vaguely wondered where my dad was, but knowing him, he was probably in the bedroom watching some sporting event. Birthday parties (especially "girly" ones) weren't his thing.

As Nikil pushed open the swinging door to the dining room, Matt and I locked eyes, and I started grinning like a crazy person as I shimmied my way toward him. When Nikil turned the conga line to go back into the living room, I peeled away and sidled up to Matt.

"Hi," I said, smiling so hard my cheeks hurt.

"Happy birthday," he said quietly as his deep dimples appeared and caused my legs to tremble. "You look really nice, Alexis."

"Thanks for coming," I said.

"I wouldn't have missed it."

We stood there grinning awkwardly.

"Did you have any cupcakes?" I asked.

"Yup. They were delicious," he said.

Grin, grin, grin.

"Oh, hey, I brought you something. Here," said Matt, pulling a small wrapped rectangular box from his back pocket and handing it to me. What could it be? A link bracelet? A necklace?

"Oh, wow! Thank you so much. You didn't need to do that," I said, my palms sweating suddenly.

"Don't be silly! It's your birthday! Go on, open it!" he said with a goofy, excited little smile.

"Okay . . . if you're sure . . . ," I said. I held the light package in my hands and chanted in my head, *Please be something I like. Please be something I like.* Unlike—*ahem*—Dylan, for example, I am a terrible faker, and the stress of having to pretend I loved something would be horrible.

My fingers were shaking as I tried to peel back the gift wrapping. I was trying to do it neatly, but Matt interrupted. "Just rip it! The lady in the store wrapped it because I am all thumbs when it comes to that stuff."

I laughed and tore off the paper, feeling giddy

when I saw what *did* look like a jewelry box. A gift of jewelry would really take things to the next level for us. Lifting the hinged lid slightly, I peeked inside to get a head start on what my reaction would be. I couldn't quite tell what kind of jewelry it was. . . . I lifted the lid entirely, and inside was . . . a wooden pen.

"Wow!" I said, exhaling.

Matt took the case from me and displayed it on his on his palm, pretending to showcase it while he jokingly gestured lavishly at it with the other hand like a salesperson. "The lady at the store said wooden accessories are very in right now. I was going to get you a pair of wooden sunglasses, but I knew you'd prefer a useful gift!"

"Thank you so much. I love it!" I said, finding his eyes and smiling warmly. But inside, my heart was crushed. I'd expected something romantic. Something that indicated he really liked me, as a girl. Not as . . . an accountant.

Matt looked at me for an extra second, and then he said, "Well, you need to get back on that dance floor with your guests, and I'm going to have one more cupcake before I have to run. I'm . . . I hope you like the pen. Happy birthday, Alexis." He put the pen back in the case and handed it to me.

"Thanks, Matt. I'll use it all the time," I said firmly. "I'm so happy you were able to make it today. I appreciate you coming." I smiled again, feeling formal and awkward. I wanted to hug him or have him hug me, but he shoved his hands into his pockets and smiled. Then he turned away, and the opportunity had passed.

I felt a lump in my throat—not like I was going to cry, but just like a chunk of disappointment was stuck there. Matt had been the person I was most excited about seeing at my party, and it hadn't gone great. It had also gone really quickly. Why had I stalled on going over to see him and say hi? Dylan wouldn't have done that if her crush had come to her party, I knew that. I walked the case back into the kitchen for safekeeping.

My mom looked up from her newspaper. "Having fun, honey?" she asked.

I nodded, suddenly wanting to cry. "It's a really nice party," I said.

"Dylan and your friends did a wonderful job. . . ."

Dylan, Dylan, Dylan. It was about her all the time!

"I know," I said. "I'm so grateful."

I stashed the pen in my book bag so I could

bring it upstairs later, and then I went back to the party, where things were beginning to wind down. Someone had lowered the volume of the music a touch, and the dining room was packed with people looking for refreshments. My dad had come through and opened the front door to let the cool air in, and the daylight washed out the disco vibe a little bit.

Dylan was easily chatting away, cracking people up and gesturing expansively. I smiled and looked around, accepting compliments like "Great party, Alexis!" and "Thanks for having me!" I couldn't claim any credit for either of those things so I just smiled and nodded and didn't break stride.

I'd had a really nice time, but now I was tired and wanted to go lie on my bed and rest—maybe do some Sudoku.

Suddenly, my besties were at my side in the living room.

"Have you had fun?" Katie asked enthusiastically.

"Totally!" I smiled, trying to amp my energy back up.

"It's been a great party," said Mia.

"Thank you so much. It's a total blast, and I loved all the thoughtful touches. You guys must've put a lot of time and effort into this. It shows."

We had a group hug, and I was grateful that no one mentioned Dylan. I'd obviously thank her later, in private.

Suddenly, the lights came up and the disco birthday song started blaring "It's your birthday, it's your birthday!" Dylan shimmied toward me with a cake shaped like a tall cylinder.

"Whaaat? I thought we were just having cupcakes!" I cried. There was a cardboard Roman candle flaring like a blowtorch on top of the cake. I wasn't sure how to begin to blow it out. My dad appeared with his phone for photos of Dylan presenting the cake to me, surrounded by my besties. I laughed and tried to put out the flame, but when the song ended, it fizzled out at the same time, and Dylan said, "Now for the best part!"

She put the platter down on the coffee table. Then suddenly Mia was by my side. She produced a knife and presented it to me to cut the cake.

"Dad, keep filming!" Dylan commanded.

"Is this thing going to explode?" I asked in jest.

"Maybe!" teased Dylan. "Be careful!"

I slid the knife into the cake twice, creating a small triangular wedge. Then I slowly withdrew it to put it on a plate. The inside of the cake was rainbow-colored layers, and the cake had a hollow core filled with colorful candies and sprinkles! I was awestruck. The cake *did* seem to explode onto the plate in a riot of color. Everyone oohed and aahed.

"Wow! This is incredible, Dylan!" I cried.

Dylan smiled in satisfaction. "Cakefetti! I knew you'd like that one! I got it at this new bakery I read about."

Besides being gorgeous and fun, the cake was delicious. We sliced slivers for everyone, and Dylan scooped the cakefetti onto people's pieces as she passed them around. I wished Matt had been here to see it. He likes innovations in baking as much as us Cupcakers do.

Soon after, everyone left in a flurry of "thank yous" and "best party evers," and my friends and I cleaned up the food and drinks and much of the décor. Just the lanterns were left on the ceiling, and the lights tracing the window frames. We hung out in the living room to enjoy it all as we rehashed the party. This is actually the part of parties that I like the best: nibbling on leftovers, discussing what went on, and laughing a lot.

Dylan had gone upstairs to change, and when she came back, she was holding a beautifully wrapped present.

"Ooh, gifts!" cried Katie, popping up to retrieve the pile of items for me that were on the front hall table.

There were lots of small gifts from my random "friends," impersonal but thoughtful and nice things like hand lotion and a ring holder and a pom-pom key chain. Then it was time for the presents from my closest friends.

Katie's gift was carefully wrapped in rose-patterned paper, which I tried to preserve as I opened it. I smiled at her as I got it off, and then I looked at the box in my hands. A new . . . calculator. Wow. Good times. I looked up and made myself smile at her.

"Thanks, Katie! This is so thoughtful. It's just what I need!"

Katie smiled and gestured at the box. "See, it's solar-powered. I know you have that old adding machine of your mom's, but it always needs to be plugged in. This is mobile, and you can use it at school when you aren't allowed to use your phone."

I looked down at the box. "It's perfect. Thank you so much." I set it aside and selected a small, flat box wrapped in striped paper.

"This one's from me!" said Emma, sitting up expectantly. "I got it for you in the city."

"Ooh! Goody!" I said in anticipation. I pulled off the paper and found . . . a blank book.

"It's a planner!" said Emma. "It's *so* you! Open it! See how it's got the weekly and daily action items, plus the section for long-term goals that you can carry over? And look at the cover. It's nice and bright, so you'll never forget it anywhere. Not that you ever forget things, but still."

"Wow!" I said. "It is just perfect. You're right. It's so me! Thanks so much, Em."

Emma beamed and wiggled happily.

The final present, besides Dylan's, was obviously from Mia. It was wrapped in a section of batik cloth that had been gathered up and tied with a huge floppy bow at the top. It was very stylish, like Mia.

"Nice, Mia. This is so pretty!"

She smiled. "I know you're going to be happy with this gift!"

"I'm sure I will be," I agreed as I eagerly unwrapped it to find . . . measuring cups.

Mia leaned in. "You kept saying in our last two meetings here that you said your kitchen needed new measuring cups. So, here you go! And . . . you'll be happy to know I got them on sale, so they were not pricey. Bam! You're welcome!"

"They're great. Thank you. Obviously, just what

I needed, and I bet at a great price, too."

"And now mine!" said Dylan, passing me her gift. It was a little heavy and in a cardboard box. I refrained from making a snide comment like, *Granny underpants? Vitamins? A savings account?* I wondered what other practical gift I could possibly get.

I ripped through the paper and lifted the box's top, just wanting to get it over with.

Inside was a beautiful black velvet dress. Gently, I lifted it from the box, and it softly unfurled, revealing pink, orange, and red roses embroidered all over it, with green leaves climbing the length of it.

"WOW! Dylan!" I cried. "This is so beautiful!" I popped up from my seat and held the dress against me, turning this way and that.

My friends all marveled at the dress. "Dylan has such an incredible sense of style," said Mia.

Dylan put her palms out defensively. "I know, I know, Alexis. It's got to be dry-cleaned, and that will be expensive, and where will you ever wear it, and it was probably too pricey and I should take it back and wait for it to go on sale. . . ." Dylan waved her hand dismissively. "But I just thought you had to have this dress, no matter what. It's going to look beautiful on you!"

I crossed the room and crushed her in a hug. "I love it. Thank you so much. Thank you so very much!" I got a little misty-eyed. "This was such a beautiful party, and I love my presents. You all know me so well. Thank you for such a special day."

"Group hug!" cried Katie, jumping up from the sofa. We did a big group squeeze, even with Dylan, and they sang happy birthday to me as we hugged it out.

It wasn't until later that night, when I was finally alone, that I really had time to think about my gifts.

CHAPTER 4

Team Go!

I was showered and clean, my makeup removed, teeth brushed, parents kissed, tucked into bed, and I couldn't stop thinking.

The party had been so nice, and there were all those thoughtful touches: the cake, the decorations, the red velvet cupcakes, Matt . . .

But the only thing I could think about was how boring I was and how great Dylan was. Like, my best friends gave me a calculator, a planner, and measuring cups for my *birthday*? And my crush gave me a *pen*?

Meanwhile, Dylan planned an incredible party and made me look amazing and came up with every little perfect detail.

I smacked my palms against my mattress in

frustration and rolled over, jerking my covers along with me. Why wasn't I fun and jazzy and full of creativity like Dylan? Why was I boring and practical and unfun? Why couldn't I do small talk and discover things like cakefetti and charm everyone to death?

I was tired of being the boring sister. I needed some new hobbies ASAP. And they had to be fun and cool ones. No more conga lines with the FBLA. I had to think up something *big*.

It struck me just before math class Monday morning. I was taking my notebook out of my backpack and feeling a little grumpy because I hadn't come up with a plan to be unboring, when an announcement over the PA system caught my attention.

It was a friendly and peppy girl's voice, speaking over some fun dance music. "Hey, everyone! It's Ceci Shanahan! I'm the captain of cheerleading this year, and I'd love for you to come and try out for the squad! Sign-ups are outside the cafeteria, and we start auditions today in the gym right after school. Come on out! It's lots of fun!"

Hmm, I thought. Dylan had been a cheerleader when she was here at Park Street Middle School, and she'd learned a lot from it: how to do her makeup, how to talk to boys, how to perform in front of a crowd, how to be more peppy. Maybe if I became a cheerleader, I'd loosen up a little, make a few fun friends, and get outside my comfort zone. *Why not?*

When I passed the cafeteria later on in the morning, I dashed over and put my name into the first slot I saw on the sign-up sheet. I'd just stay in my sports clothes after PE and pop into the gym for tryouts. Nothing special. I knew some routines from when I've watched Dylan cheer. I am a good dancer, so I could knock those out in my sleep. And Ceci was a really nice girl. She would set a good tone for the group, so it wouldn't be snarky. I allowed myself a tiny bit of hope as I looked forward to the tryouts after school.

Wait, whaaaaat? Did I say "hope"? Did I actually say I was looking *forward* to the tryouts? Wow.

As PE class drew to a close, more and more girls asked the teacher if they could please go to the bathroom. Since it was so late, she told them to go ahead and hit the locker room afterward and she'd see them next time. By the time the bell rang, I was one of the only girls left in gym. I soon found out why.

The bathroom was jammed with girls in cute

short skirts and fitted tops, slathering on makeup and hair-spraying their strands into elaborate coifs. I choked and waved the air in front of my face as I tried to walk through the cloud of body sprays and perfumes. The chatter was at a high decibel level, ricocheting off the tiles, which amplified the noise to a deafening roar. Everyone was discussing cheer tryouts. Apparently, people had heard rumors about the upcoming tryouts and had been practicing for weeks, studying routines on YouTube and ordering outfits from Amazon.

I was in way over my head.

I quickly used the bathroom and went back to my gym locker to grab my things. I had on a pair of sweats and a T-shirt, my usual gym attire. I hadn't thought anything of it earlier, but now it was clear I was wildly underdressed. As I exited the locker room, I made a beeline to cross my name off the schedule, but the sign-up sheet was gone! Someone had already removed it from the bulletin board. I leaned back against the board and closed my eyes, rolling my head from side to side.

Should I just go home without crossing my name off the list? Would Ceci stand there calling my name? How many times would she call for me before she realized I wasn't there? Would everyone then know I'd chickened out? What should I do?

As I stood there paralyzed, watching people stream into the gym, suddenly, Ceci herself popped her head out of the double doors to scan the hallway for latecomers. She spotted me and walked over.

"Hey, Alexis! I'm so happy you're coming out today! I've seen your sister cheer, and it would be an honor to have another Becker on the squad!" She smiled in a warm and welcoming fashion, her blue eyes twinkling, and then I saw her notice my outfit. She was too kind to say anything critical, but she hesitated. "We're just about to get started. Are you all set?"

I didn't know what else to do. I couldn't figure out how to get out of it. It was like I was already strapped into the roller coaster, and I just had to go on the ride in order to get out the other side.

"Yup. I guess so," I said, pushing myself off the bulletin board.

"Come on in, then. We'll get things going on time today."

I followed Ceci blindly, her long, reddish brown curls bouncing and glinting, and I regretted having done absolutely nothing with my hair.

"Ceci!" I grabbed her in a panic, and she turned, a look of concern on her face.

"Are you okay, Alexis?"

I took a deep breath through my nose. "I . . . I hadn't known about the tryouts today, so I'm . . . I don't have an outfit. . . . I didn't bring anything for my . . . hair or makeup or anything. . . ." I gestured to my face.

Ceci smiled and linked her arm through mine comfortingly. "Alexis, these girls watch too much TV. We are not a glamour squad. We're just here to have fun and celebrate our players together. You're so naturally pretty, and I think you're smart to be comfortably dressed for tryouts. Some of those girls' shirts are so tight, they won't be able to even lift their arms. She gave my shoulder a squeeze. "I know you'll be great. Don't worry. Just remember to breathe. Like, start now. . . ." She laughed.

I sighed heavily. "Okay. Okay. I'll . . . I can try. I . . . How long do I have before I go on?" I figured I could watch a couple of girls and then go out in the hall to practice a bit before I went on.

Ceci bit her lip and looked at me kindly. "Alexis, you signed up to go first."

I felt the blood drain from my face. "I did?"

Ceci nodded. "I can push you to the end of the list, but sometimes, if we run over, the janitor shuts us down and we won't have time to see you. You're really better off going first and getting it over with."

Now it was my turn to bite my lip.

Ceci leaned in and spoke softly and calmly to me. "Listen, my little brother, John, has some special needs, and we always have him do a few yoga poses when he's wound up. Do you know any? You could do them as warm-ups?"

"Maybe . . ." She had a point. I did know a few. . . .

"What does Dylan do before she cheers? Did she ever share her training or warm-ups with you?"

My heart sank. "Probably. I just can't remember. It's okay. I'll just go ahead and do my routine, for better or for worse."

Ceci looked at me earnestly, her blue eyes pooling with concern. "Are you sure?"

I exhaled quickly. "Yup. I'm just going to do what I came to do, and then I'll be moving along. Thanks, Ceci. I really appreciate your help."

She smiled warmly. "You're going to be great. I know it. Don't worry."

"Thanks."

I walked over to the bleachers to stow my stuff, and as I did, who should come flouncing past but Olivia Allen, our grade's resident mean girl. She passed me, and then she did a theatrical double take, like superexaggerated, while clutching her chest.

"*Alexis Becker?* At cheer tryouts? You can't be serious?" She scanned the crowd to see if she could catch anyone's eye, presumably so they could laugh at me together, but no one was looking at her. She looked back down at me. "Hoping you've got a little of your sister's mojo? Or maybe just some goodwill from the organizers? You know, Alexis, you can't ride on Dylan's coattails forever." And she marched away.

Great.

Ceci stepped up in front of the judges' table with a megaphone. She was friendly, poised, and confident.

"Hey, girls! Welcome! I'm Ceci Shanahan, and I am so happy to see you all out here today for cheering! We're going to have lots of fun, but the most important thing is to be kind to one another. Everyone's taking a risk today, putting themselves out here, and cheerleading is all about encouragement! So, I want to see you supporting your fellow cheerleaders, okay?"

The crowd went wild, obviously demonstrating their cheering abilities.

Just then the gym doors opened, and the entire boys' basketball team entered single file and climbed the bleachers. I couldn't look, but I knew Matt's buddy Greg had to be there. I'd forgotten that Dylan had once told me they had a tradition where the boys' teams watched the girls' cheerleading tryouts each season.

Just when I though it couldn't get any worse! My palms were actively sweating now.

Ceci laughed and said into her megaphone, "Hi, boys! Thanks for coming. Just reminding our group here that this is a supportive atmosphere, and cheerleading is about telling people they are doing a greeeeeaaaaaat job!" Ceci pumped her fist in the air and the crowd went wild again. She quieted them down and reached back to the table for her clipboard.

"Okay, today we're starting with Alexis Becker. Alexis is so brave to go first, but that's because she's a great dancer. Please give it up for Alexis!"

The bleachers exploded, and somehow my brain propelled my body onto my feet, which started walking toward the judges' table. Ceci handed me two pom-poms, and I took my spot on the X taped on the floor.

I stood there for a few seconds, trying to breathe, staring out at the crowd, searching for Greg but finding Olivia Allen instead. She was snickering at me. Maybe it was just a smile, but it looked like a snicker. I had never been so underprepared for something in my *life*. It was totally unlike me to wing anything.

Ceci whispered from behind me, "Whenever you're ready, Alexis. You can do it!"

Oh, why didn't I make a list of moves I have seen Dylan do? Why didn't I tell my friends—they would have talked me out of it! What do I even cheer about? What would Dylan do?

That's what finally got me moving. I just channeled Dylan.

I lifted my pom-poms into the air and started marching in place. I began with the usual chant: "Ready . . . okay. Here we go! Give me a *T*!"

There was silence.

"They can't hear you," whispered Ceci, coaching from behind me. "Be louder. Like really loud!"

"Okay, give me a *T*!" I bellowed.

The crowd yelled, *"T!"*

Whoa! Okay.

"Give me an *E*!"

"E!"

"Give me an *A*!"

"A!"

"Give me a *M*!"

47

"M!"

"Give me a G!"

"G!"

"Give me an O!"

"O!"

"What does that spell?"

The crowd didn't respond. So I did a twirl and yelled, "Team go!"

Wait, what? What *did* I just spell?

"Go, team!" I corrected.

"Go, team!" cheered the crowd.

Meanwhile, throughout all this, I was stomping and spelling out each letter with the pom-poms while shaking my hips, like I'd seen Dylan do a million times. But I'd reached the end of my cheer and I couldn't think of anything else. Like my mind was literally as dry and blank as a desert. I kept kind of marching in place for a minute and shaking the pom-poms, but that was all I had. Finally, I gave them one last big shake, and I turned and put them down on the judges' table.

"Nice job, Alexis," Ceci said with an encouraging smile. The other two judges just looked confused, like *Was that all?*

My face was purple with embarrassment as I walked quickly back to the bleachers to grab my things. Somehow Olivia had sidled down next to my spot while I was cheering.

"I can't even believe you're Dylan Becker's sister! She'd die of shame if she'd seen that!" she said in her usual nasty little tone.

I glared at her, but I couldn't trust my voice to say anything. I cast one last hopeless glance back toward the boys' basketball team. I looked up into the stands and happen to catch Greg's eye. He gave me a little wave, but his face said it all: *What was that about?*

I made it out of the school, dramatically smashing through the double doors and stalking to my bike in the rack, without crying. But as soon as I strapped on my helmet and began to pedal, the tears started to flow. Always one to be cautious, I pedaled a bit slower than usual because of my tears.

Of all the dumb ideas! What was I thinking? I shuddered, picturing the looks on people's faces as they waited for me to continue and then realized that I wasn't. I wiped my cheek on my shoulder. I couldn't wait to get home.

What was I going to do now to become peppier and more fun? I'd been the center of attention today, just like Dylan usually is, but it was for all the wrong reasons, and it was my own fault.

As soon as I got home, I did the only thing I could think of to make myself feel better. I got into a nice hot bath and . . . pretended I was a duck again—and let the day roll off my back.

CHAPTER 5

Branching Out

$\mathcal{I}$ would have stayed home sick the next day except I had an FBLA meeting after school and a quiz prep in Spanish that I didn't want to miss. Instead, I wore a hat and my glasses instead of contacts, and I kept a low profile, hoping no one would say anything to me about the tryouts. I avoided eye contact in the halls and stayed mum in my classes, which was very unlike me.

At lunch, Katie looked at me with concern. "Are you feeling well, Alexis?"

I looked up from under the brim of my hat. "Hmm? Oh. Yeah. Fine. Just a little . . . um, tired."

Katie and Mia exchanged glances.

"You look like you're trying to be incognito," said Mia.

"Oh really?" I said breezily. "That's funny. Ha-ha. Like, why would I want to do that?"

What the heck, I decided. I took the hat off and shook out my hair. Just then an underclassman was passing by.

"Nice job yesterday, Alexis," she said, wide-eyed at her own daring in speaking to someone in a grade above her.

All three Cupcakers' heads swiveled toward me. I shrugged, putting my palms in the air. "No idea what that kid is talking about," I said.

I busied myself with what scraps of food were left on my tray.

"Alexis!" Emma said in her warning voice.

I looked up, all innocence. "What?"

"What are you not telling us?"

"Me?"

Emma nodded and pointed her finger at me. "Yes, you, missy. Why was she complimenting you?"

"Oh, that." I waved my hand breezily. "You know . . ."

Katie laughed. "No! We *don't* know! That's why we're asking. What's up?"

I looked at the three of them, my very best friends, all searching me carefully. How could I lie to them? I took a deep breath.

"I tried out for cheerleading yesterday," I said, and then I shrugged again. "That's all. No biggie."

"Whaaat? *You?* Cheerleading?" Emma's jaw was practically on the cafeteria floor.

I had to laugh a little, but I was also indignant. "Yeah, so? Why not? It's my family legacy." I stuck out my chin in defiance.

Emma sat back in her chair in shock. "I thought you always said cheering was ridiculous and a waste of time."

"Well, maybe I used to, but now I'm more mature, and with that maturity comes a certain . . ."

Mia smacked her palm on the table. "Wait. I know! You're trying to become more like Dylan. Isn't she?" She turned to our friends, and her eyebrows raised in a questioning fashion.

"Who, me? Like Dylan? Why?"

Mia shook her head. "I don't know, but you were complaining about Dylan over the weekend, and now you're trying out for her trademark activity? Something you always claimed—"

"To hate!" interrupted Emma, laughing. "Is Mia right? Are you trying to be more like Dylan?"

"Look, I'm just . . ."

"Hey, way to go yesterday, Alexis Becker," said some random sixth-grade boy I've never seen before. He laughed as he rejoined his friends at their table.

"Okay. You have to tell us everything," Mia said.

I sighed and told them. They were silent for a minute afterward.

"Well . . . ," said Emma, folding and unfolding her fingers.

"I bet it wasn't as bad as you think," Katie said finally, patting my hand comfortingly.

"Actually, it might have been worse," I said.

"Look, you just need to get back in the saddle. Try something else. Keep moving forward."

"Like what?" I asked.

"You can come to fashion club with me," offered Mia. "Or my sewing group?"

"Umm . . ." Dylan is really into fashion, so maybe that would be a good route for me to take. It's not an interest of mine, but I could fake it. Fake it till you make it. That could be a new motto for me, right?

"Want to come work in my mom's office with me after school one day?" suggested Katie. "You could do billing . . . ," she said tantalizingly. I do love a good invoicing session, but that was the usual me. I wanted to break into new territory and try new things, things that would make me peppy and appealing and fun and overall more Dylan-ish.

"Why don't you come running with me later?" offered Emma. She likes to stay in shape for sports and also for work, so she runs three miles a few times a week.

Hmm. I could be a runner. That was one thing I could do. Easily. Everyone can run. And runners were cool and mature—very sophisticated. They were always all "Not now. I have to go for my *run!*" And everyone would wait for them until they came back from carving out their Me Time. Dylan was a runner sometimes. And Katie loves to run too.

"Okay," I agreed.

"Great. Meet me at my house at four o'clock."

"Oh." I didn't want to have to see Matt. What if his friend Greg told him about the tryouts? There was no way I was going to the Taylors' house. "Can't you come to me, please?"

"It's not really on my route," she said. "I have the distance all paced out. My dad did it in his car for me."

"Just this once?" I asked.

Emma sighed. "Okay. I guess. But it will be a little later. I'll see you at four forty, okay?"

"Thanks," I said.

Just then Ceci passed me on her way to dump

her lunch tray. "Hey, Alexis! I've been looking for you. Thanks for coming to tryouts yesterday!"

Good thing I'd just told my friends or they would have needed CPR just then.

"Thanks for having me," I said quietly. "Sorry I was such a . . ."

Ceci shook her head. "We ran out of time yesterday, so we have to have another session today. I'd love to have you come back if you want to try anything else? I know you got kind of cut short . . . ?"

That was such a kind way of putting it, but I had to shut this down.

"Thanks, Ceci. That is so nice of you. Really. I just think . . . I mean, there are girls there who really, really must be talented, so I think I'll just bow out now."

Ceci looked at me carefully. "Are you sure?"

I nodded. "Yup. I'm sure. It was kind of a lark anyway."

Ceci sighed. "Okay, well, if you ever decide you want to join, you just come and find me, okay? People get injured; we always need subs if people have to go away, you know. . . . You'd be a great addition to the crew. We need nice girls who can dance, that's all! You can easily learn the rest! Bye!"

"Thanks so much, Ceci! Bye!"

"That girl is so nice," said Katie, shaking her head in admiration.

"Yeah, if she was in our grade, she'd be my best friend . . . ," Emma said wistfully.

"Hey!" I said, whacking her on the arm.

"Oh, I mean if she was and you weren't!" Emma laughed.

"That's enough out of you, missy. See you after school."

At four forty on the nose, Emma appeared in my driveway. I was sitting on my front stoop, all decked out in my athletic gear, shoes tied, the works. I jogged down the steps and across the grass to join her.

"All stretched out?" she asked between gasps.

"What? Oh. I'm good. I'm pretty limber. You know."

She looked at me skeptically. "Okay. . . ."

"Let's go!" I said, all perky.

Emma jogged in a U-turn, and I followed, moving beside her and trying to match the rhythm of my steps to hers. It was kind of awkward. We're both pretty tall, but I like to take big steps, and she was taking these little baby shuffle steps.

"Why are you running like this?" I asked. "It's not really running."

Emma shrugged. "It's what I do," she said breathlessly.

I ran next to her in silence. It was boring. After a block or so, I said, "Why don't you listen to music when you do this?"

"Distracts me," said Emma.

"From what?" I pressed.

"My thoughts."

"Hmm."

I was quiet for a moment, just shuffling along. But I was so bored! How could Dylan and Emma enjoy this hobby?

"If you could live anywhere on Earth, where would it be?" I asked.

Emma stopped running and stood with her hands on her hips, panting. "Lex, here's how I run: I start running in silence, I run the whole time in silence, and then I go home."

"Okay!" I said. "Is that a hint?"

Emma laughed and shook her head. "It's a request. A firm one. Let's not talk, okay?"

"Okay, okay!"

We started running again—shuffling, I mean. I looked around, talked to myself in my head, tried to count to a thousand, quizzed myself on my Spanish, and became more bored. Maybe if I had music or if I were running fast, like actually running, this would be good. Maybe if my running companion was chatty, or whatever, it would be fun. But I could already say after five blocks that jogging with Emma was not for me.

"Em?"

"Mmm-hmm?"

"I'm going home."

"Okay. Later."

"Thanks for having me," I said. And I did a U-turn and sprinted home at full speed, which left me breathless for like twenty minutes.

The next day Mia insisted I come to her fashion club meeting after school. Seeing as how Dylan is obsessed with fashion and has repeatedly helped me with choosing outfits, I thought this maybe wasn't the worst idea. If I could become a tiny bit more fashionable, I'd be on my way to being more like Dylan.

The club met in the library, a place I am very comfortable in. The librarian greeted me warmly, and I felt like I was off to a great start.

Ms. Rumbough is the faculty adviser for the

group. She was an art teacher who had lived and worked in the city before, and she always dressed like she was going to the opening of a fancy art show—thick black-framed glasses, a tight ponytail, severe outfits that were all angles, mostly in black, and clompy black shoes or boots, depending on the season. I always found her intimidating, but I'd never had a class with her.

There were seven kids in the meeting today—three boys and four girls, including me. Ms. Rumbough passed around library books that had been flagged with Post-It notes, and talked to us about a designer named Christian Dior and the New Look he came up with in the 1940s and 1950s. It was pretty interesting, actually, and the clothes in the books were cool—fitted button-down shirts with flared pleated skirts. After her chat, which lasted about twenty minutes, Ms. Rumbough handed around drawing paper and colored pencils and instructed us to create some sketches for outfits in the New Look style.

Um.

Everyone else eagerly set to the task, as if Ms. Rumbough's talk had been the boring part, and now they were finally being unleashed to do what they'd come here for. I, on the other hand, felt paralyzed and overwhelmed. I didn't have the slightest idea of how to begin, and instead wished Ms. Rumbough would keep teaching us interesting historical stuff.

I stared at my paper and sighed.

"Having a tough time finding inspiration?" Ms. Rumbough asked gently.

I nodded. "I'm not the creative type," I said.

Ms. Rumbough smiled. "Everyone has creativity. It's just figuring out what things inspire you. A lot of designers start with the fabric. They choose new fabrics and let the textures and folds of the fabric dictate their designs."

That made sense.

"Other designers are inspired by color. They pick a palette for the season and work within those parameters. Still, others just like to draw. Maybe they're inspired by something they saw in art, or on the street—even in architecture or food. You never know what will inspire you. You might keep a file of things you think are cool and then pull it out for inspiration when you need it."

"Okay," I agreed. I wondered what inspired Dylan in the world of fashion.

"You can also just doodle. Sometimes that gets the juices flowing."

"Thanks," I said. She was really nice, and this was all interesting. I'd give it a try. I knew if Dylan were here, she'd be sketching away, her colored pencils scratching quickly over the paper, covering sheet after sheet with her brilliant clothing ideas.

I glanced over at Mia. She was totally into her sketching. I looked at her pad. She had already drawn three amazing outfits!

I started doodling hearts, then flowers. I tried to do a drawing of my cat, Puff, but it looked like a mouse. I peeked at other people's work, and from what I could see, they were incredible. Ms. Rumbough went from kid to kid, offering support or helping with problem-solving. Dylan would have adored this, but the truth was, I didn't. I sat for two more minutes and then decided I needed to get out of there, like immediately. I felt trapped.

I gathered my things and crumpled my drawings and tossed them into the trash. Then I stood and walked over to Ms. Rumbough. "Thank you so much for having me today, Ms. Rumbough. I loved your talk. I have to run now. Bye!" And I took off, mouthing at Mia that I'd call her later.

Outside school, I let out a deep breath. "Phew!" I felt like I'd escaped from prison. Fashion design was not for me.

❧

The next day Katie texted me first thing in the morning. She wrote: Have to go to mall after school for baking stuff. Want to come and we can check out new makeup store?

Hmm. I am not a makeup person, but Dylan is. And neither was Katie until recently. She had a modeling assignment, and now every once in a while she gets the urge to check out makeup counters—just for fun. Maybe I'd find something in there that would get me started on the road to cosmetic expertise. Yes, I typed back. Then Thanks, I added.

Katie's mom picked us up after school and took us to the mall. "I have a patient in twenty minutes, who will take an hour or so. I'll pick you up in an hour and a half, okay, girls?"

"Perfect," agreed Katie.

Once at the mall, Katie led me directly to Baker's Hollow, the baking supply store where we spend lots of time (and money that we earn for the Cupcake Club). The manager actually knows Katie by name, so we had to chat with her for a while first. She showed us some beautiful new edible glitter toppings in jewel tones, and I spied jars of cakefetti for sale and pointed them out to

Katie. We agreed it would be fun to figure out how to do exploding cupcakes, so we bought two small jars of the cakefetti to experiment with. (Two small jars had more ounces of cakefetti, at a lower price, than the large jar, I was proud to note.) We got smoothies at the food court, and then we went to check out the new store, Lit Beauty.

Lit Beauty was massive, with all different zones for skin care, hair care, hairstyling, body care, body art, nails, perfumes, sunscreens, and more. One cool thing they had were these little private stalls where you could duck inside, pull the curtain closed, and see your makeup in different kinds of lighting, just by pushing a button.

Katie and I put on dark purple lipstick and then went inside one of the stalls to see it in tropical dawn, high noon, evening mist, black light, candlelight, and more. It was so much fun.

There were tons of salespeople milling around, offering to do things to you, and Katie and I let them. We got silver feather tattoos on our arms, and tiny jewels glued to the tops of our cheekbones, and ringlets curled into our hair, and perfume samples up and down our arms. Someone offered to "shape" our eyebrows, but I remembered Dylan's cautions of "redness and swelling," and we declined.

Katie got a mini makeover with a smoky eye and a pale lip. I got one with subtle eyes and a strong lip. By the time we had to meet Katie's mom, we had been smoothed, glossed, brightened, curled, enhanced, and scented within an inch of our lives. I couldn't wait to hear what Dylan thought when she saw me at home.

Katie's mom raised her eyebrows and then sneezed when we got into the car. We all laughed.

"How do we look?" asked Katie, batting her eyelash extensions at her mom.

"Inappropriate! Oh, Alexis, your mom is going to kill me!" Katie's mom laughed.

"It's okay. My sister, Dylan, is really into makeup, so my mom is used to this."

But that wasn't totally true. My mom put up with Dylan's experimenting while in the house, but Dylan was never allowed out with much makeup on. I imagined she wasn't going to be too happy when she saw me.

My mom took one look at me when I got home—this is the woman who barely let me wear clear mascara to my own birthday party—and jerked her thumb toward the bathroom. "Off!" she ordered.

"Why? Don't I look beautiful?" I trilled.

"Yes, without all that junk on you."

I passed Dylan in the upstairs hall, and she looked me over from head to toe.

"Cool tattoo," she said.

That was all?

Ugh. My eyes would be red and stinging from the makeup remover all night now, and nobody even thought my makeover looked fabulous.

Time for a different hobby.

CHAPTER 6

Family Roles

$\mathcal{I}$ had made it through the week without having to see Matt. Normally, this would be a terrible thing, but after the awkward gift thing at my party and then the cheer tryouts, I was avoiding him like the plague.

Our meeting this week was on Friday, since we were all so busy. It was scheduled to be at Emma's, but at lunch that day, I requested a change of location.

"Alexis, you've been acting strange all week. You usually love coming over to my house and trying to see if Matt will be home. Are you avoiding him? Do you not like him anymore?" Emma asked. "Did something happen at your party?"

I thought fast. "Of course I still like him, but

you know the saying—'Absence makes the heart grow fonder.'"

Emma looked at me skeptically for a second, but then she shrugged. "Okay, whatever, I guess. Where should we meet?"

We agreed to come to my house so I could break in my new measuring cups. Emma had the contact info now for the talent show manager, who said he was interested in a cupcake sale, so we would put together a good proposal for that too. We had just one event this weekend to bake for, besides Mona's minis. It was for a baby shower in the neighborhood, and the cupcakes were super-basic. Today would be easy.

After school, we walked together to my house. When we got there, I saw that Dylan was already home. I prayed she wouldn't come downstairs and take over my Cupcake Club meeting.

We laid out all the ingredients and supplies for Mona's minis and began baking. I made a big deal out of pitching our old measuring cups into the recycling bin, and ceremoniously asking everyone to bless our new measuring cups, asking for strength, accuracy, and the ability to not go missing.

"And please magically convert gluten to cash," I added, and everyone laughed.

As we were laughing, Dylan came down the back stairs. "Hey! Alexis, what's the deal with cheerleading?" she said by way of greeting.

"Hi, Dylan!" my friends all singsonged. Yuck. But she ignored them.

"What are you talking about?" I replied, all innocent.

"I ran into Ceci Shanahan—cute kid, by the way—and she told me you'd tried out for cheerleading this week? I said she had to be mistaken, there was no way Alexis would try out for cheering without consulting me for training and tips." Dylan stood with her hands on her hips, glaring at me.

My friends looked nervously between us.

I busied myself with measuring out some flour and played it all casual. "Well, it was just a fact-finding mission. Like exploratory. You know. No biggie." I shrugged.

I could feel Dylan still staring at me.

"Alexis, I was cheer captain for two years. I can't imagine that you would try out and not ask for my help. I'm practically a professional. What did you do for your routine? What songs did you do it to? What did you wear? Did you just figure everything out on your own?"

I glared at her. "Dylan, we are in the middle of

a Cupcake Club meeting now, so maybe we could discuss this later." *Like,* much *later,* I thought.

"All I know is that if you didn't make the squad, it's your own fault for not seeking my help, because it's not something you'd be able to do on your own!" Dylan harrumphed and then spun on her heel and left the room.

My friends were silent for a moment.

"So, that was awkward . . . ," I said with a laugh.

"Maybe I'm *sometimes* glad I don't have an older sister . . . ?" ventured Katie, which broke the ice.

Mia gasped, "Wow, I know you always say Dylan can be mean, but I've never seen it before."

I shrugged. "Stick around."

"I've seen it a lot, but I thought she'd grown out of it," said Emma. "She was so nice to us when we were planning your party."

"Yeah, but that's because you were all, like, her little fan club, worshiping her," I said.

"I guess," agreed Emma. "Well, big brothers can be just as bad, worse even—because they'll do things like pick you up and lock you in the closet."

"Matt wouldn't do that!" I protested, rising to his defense immediately.

Emma rolled her eyes. "He might. He does it to Jake sometimes. But Sam's the one who invented it.

He calls it 'Quiet Time.'" Sam was Emma's oldest brother. He was nice, but he was so old, like eighteen, that we barely ever saw him.

Katie's eyes were wide with fear. "I couldn't take that. I hate the dark!"

Emma laughed. "You get used to it. The more of a fuss you make, the more they do it, so you just have to kind of tough it out and the appeal wears off. My mom taught me that. She had four older brothers. Can you imagine?" She shuddered.

I couldn't imagine having even one, and Emma had two older brothers!

"What else do they do?" asked Mia. She only has a stepbrother, Daniel, and he's nice to us—and Mia.

"One thing they like to do to me is call friends of theirs and tell them I have a crush on them." Emma rolled her eyes.

"That is awful! Does Matt do that?" I asked.

"Mm-hmm," Emma said with a nod. "Or they'll hold my things over the toilet, like they're going to drop them into the water, unless I do what they say."

"Wow!" Katie was traumatized.

"I guess having siblings is a little overrated, right, Katie?" said Mia.

They laughed.

71

"Totally," said Katie. "Although, I'll have more feedback on this after my mom gets married and Emily becomes my stepsister."

"Yeah, and at least you're not being compared to people all the time," said Emma.

"Wait, how can *you* be compared?" I asked in surprise. "They're all boys!"

"So?" said Emma. "My parents do it all the time. They pretend they're not, but they sneak it in. Like 'Oh, Sam's so responsible with his schedule; he never forgets appointments,' or 'Matt has always done so well in Spanish; I can't understand why you don't.' Stuff like that."

"Really?" I said, propping my elbows on the counter and leaning my chin on the heel of my palm. This was fascinating stuff. How had Emma and I never discussed this before?

Emma nodded. "Sam's the worst because they think he's Mr. Perfect."

Mia looked bewildered. "Anyone would think you were perfect too, with all you do."

Emma shrugged. "It's just different in families. You get a role, and it's hard to break out. I'm the unreliable one."

"Whaaat? That's insane!" said Mia, smacking the counter. "Why? How?"

Emma laughed. "I don't know. I guess I went through a phase where I forgot a bunch of stuff and, like, left the oven on once, or whatever. It's not even accurate anymore. It's just the role I play in my family. It's what they all think."

Hmmm, I thought. *Kind of like Dylan being the "fun one"?*

"Anyway, it's boring," said Emma, brushing it off. "I'm used to it by now."

Katie came over and hugged Emma. "I think you're very reliable," she said.

"Thanks." Emma smiled. "Enough about my annoying family. Let's get this talent show proposal going. Alexis, what do you think we should do?"

I stood up, filing away Emma's commentary to think about later.

"Okay, I've been thinking about this since you even mentioned it might be a possibility. We'll do very simple cupcakes that will appeal to anyone—vanilla base and half with chocolate frosting and half with vanilla. Then we'll have five little dishes of toppings for customizing, just like you had at my party, but mostly low cost: gummy bears, crushed Oreos, M&M's, cakefetti, and chopped strawberries. We'll need two people to run the station, plus a cash box, paper goods, and something like a paper and pen or a tablet to keep track of sales. The paper goods should have a theme like the show, maybe with musical notes or Hollywood stars on them or something. For quantity, I'm thinking if there are probably twenty-five kids in the show, and they each have at least one adult there, so that's fifty people, plus maybe thirty more for miscellaneous people like teachers and siblings. So, we could make around eight dozen cupcakes. We'll charge two dollars a cupcake; three dollars if they want to customize. We'll donate twenty-five percent of the profits to the school for charity. If we sell out—assuming half the people want the three-dollar-topping option—we will make about one hundred and eighty dollars, then subtract the costs, so probably around a one-hundred-and-twenty- or one-hundred-and-thirty-dollar profit. That's all."

Everyone was staring at me when I finished.

"What?" I asked, blinking.

"You're incredible," said Mia, shaking her head with a look of wonder on her face.

"How do you just . . . spin that stuff out like that? Like map out a whole proposal off the top of your head? You didn't forget anything," Katie said in amazement.

"And all that math!" added Mia.

"It's nothing," I said. "Come on. You guys are being weird."

"It's pretty impressive, Lex," agreed Emma. "You are such a clear thinker. So organized."

"Ugh." I shuddered. "I am so tired of being organized and practical and businesslike and whatever else! I want to be fun and peppy and social and creative and wild!" I threw my hands into the air and spun in a circle. When I stopped, my friends were exchanging puzzled glances.

"But *why?*" asked Katie. "You're so great at everything you're great at. Why try to be great at everything?"

Because Dylan is? I wanted to say, but I didn't. "Um, because the Beckers try harder?" That's our family motto, which all my friends know (and tease me about since it used to be a car rental's motto).

"Well, you're great just as you are, and I think that plan sounds perfect. You've thought of everything. If you can type it up just like that and send it, I'm sure the school will let us sell cupcakes at the event," said Mia.

"Totally," Emma agreed with a firm nod.

"Great!" I exclaimed. "Now let's do those baby shower cupcakes."

❖

After our session, and with Mona's minis and the baby shower cupcakes stacked neatly in our cupcake carriers, my friends left. We had plans for the next day to see a movie, and I was looking forward to getting my homework out of the way. I was in the middle of a math proof when my mom called us down to dinner.

"Mmm, broiled teriyaki salmon!" I said, sliding into a chair. "Smells delish!"

"Thank you, sweetheart," said my mom.

Dylan appeared, her face still stormy like before, and my dad sat down, shook out his napkin, and put it across his lap. Then he looked at her. "Everything okay, Dilly?" He glanced at my mom, and she shook her head a little to show she had no idea what was going on.

I looked down at my plate. Was this going to be some Dylan fit about the cheerleading?

Dylan gave an aggravated sigh. "Did you know Alexis was trying out for cheerleading at school?"

My parents turned to me with surprised looks on their faces. "Why, that's wonderful, Alexis! When are the tryouts?" asked my dad.

"I'm sure Dylan will be a big help to you!" said my mom, smiling at both of us.

Dylan glared at me. "Well, I *would* have been if

someone had asked me before she just went ahead willy-nilly and tried out!"

My mom's eyebrows went up. "Oh, the tryouts already happened?"

I shrugged. "Yeah. They were the other day."

"How did it go?" asked my dad.

"Badly. I didn't make it," I said, taking a bit of salmon onto my fork and putting it into my mouth. "It's okay," I mumbled.

"Don't talk with your mouth full, dear," scolded my mom. "Why didn't you ask Dylan for help? She's a wonderful cheerleader!" My mom beamed at Dylan, who continued to scowl at me.

"Yeah, why didn't you ask Dylan for help?" grumbled Dylan.

I swallowed and put my fork down. "Look, it was a spontaneous decision. I did a bad job, but it was my decision."

"Well, now people think the Beckers can't cheer, so your decision does affect me."

"Why does everything always have to be Dylan, Dylan, Dylan!" I cried, flinging my napkin onto the table.

"Okay, settle down, now, girls. Please finish your dinner nicely, and we will discuss it afterward. There are obviously a lot of strong feelings here, and I'd like to enjoy my meal in peace," my father said in his rarely used stern voice. He looked at my mother. "And how was your day today, dear?"

I took a deep breath and gulped down my dinner, and then I asked if I could please be excused. I put my plate in the dishwasher and stomped back up to my room.

After a bit, my mom knocked softly on the door. "What?" I said flatly.

She pushed the door open a little. "May I come in, please?"

I sighed and closed my math book, then swiveled in my chair to look at her. "What?"

"I just wanted to talk to you about what happened with cheerleading and if you're okay with it. I also wanted to apologize. Dad and I did make it all about Dylan, and we're sorry."

Whoa! That was a shocker! "Are you serious?" I asked.

My mom nodded. "We realized that lately we've talked her up too much, and it was wrong of us."

"Well, she is *perfect*!" I said sarcastically.

My mom shook her head. "No one's perfect. And you never know what's going on in someone's life that can make them react certain ways. Like right now Dylan's feeling a little insecure at school, and Dad and I are building her up, trying to make her feel better."

"Wait, what?" You could have knocked me over with a feather. "What does Dylan have to feel insecure about?"

My mom shrugged. "I think Dylan wants to keep that private for now, but just know that Dylan and her life are certainly not perfect. We did not mean to give you the impression that we think she is, in any way." My mom looked down at her hands. "You know, when I was your age and dancing twenty-four seven, I would always compare myself to the other dancers. It's the ballet way of life—you feel like you're never enough. Never thin enough, never graceful enough, never disciplined enough. It's almost like modeling—it makes you crazy about factors you sometimes can't control, like the bend of your kneecaps!" My mom laughed. "Boy, was I insecure about my knees!" She looked down at her legs. "The time I wasted worrying about these knobby little guys . . . !"

I laughed. "Seriously, Mom?"

"Yes, and these two older girls were always being held up by our teachers as having the prettiest turnouts and lines, and they had these perfect hyperextended knees. . . ."

"Mom, you sound like a crazy person!"

"Exactly!" She laughed. "See what I mean? Don't try to be someone you're not or force yourself into things that are not *your* passions."

I thought of the cheerleading (cringe fest) and the running and fashion club and the makeup, and I slowly nodded. "It's just that I'm so boring. I mean, I got measuring cups and a calculator for my birthday . . . *from my best friends!*"

My mom patted my leg. "You're lucky your friends know you so well. Imagine how furious you would have been if they'd given you expensive hair product or some frivolous scarf or something. You'd say your very best friends didn't know you at all!"

I had to laugh. "True."

"And you'd be mad that they overspent! You'd probably track down the same item somewhere else for less money, just to prove a point to them!"

Now I was really laughing. "You got me there!"

"Look, you have strong interests and talents in business and also in ballroom dance. You know, there are even colleges that have competitive ballroom-dance teams."

"Really?"

My mom nodded. "If you're looking to be a better you, why don't you focus on the things you love? Get even more immersed in them? And maybe there are one or two other things you've always enjoyed but haven't spent the time on. Think about that for a bit too."

I nodded slowly. "Okay. Will you help me come up with a plan?"

"I'd love to," agreed my mom.

"Thanks, Mom."

"Love you, sweetheart. Just focus on being the best Alexis you can be. That's all we could ever hope for."

After she left, I took a homework break and went over to my new planner from Emma. I actually preferred it to my bulky old one. It was useful *and* stylish.

I looked at the goals list and long-term projects column, and I wrote "Ballroom Dance." Then I wrote "Business Skills Development." I wanted to add one more thing, just to be well-rounded, but I wasn't sure what.

I closed the book, satisfied for the moment, and returned to my desk for my homework. I hated wasting potential study time on a weekend. After all, my family role was "the organized one."

CHAPTER 7

Surprises

The next morning I got up early and wrote the proposal for the talent show cupcakes and sent it off. It was only six days away, so we needed a quick commitment in order to slot it into our baking schedule.

Then I got out my planner and brainstormed for an additional hobby—something that might become my trademark or my passion. Something that would be all mine, not Dylan's. I tried to think of things I'd really enjoyed doing over the years, and I made a list:

> Working on my mom's
> dollhouse
> . redecorate it with her?

Learning a dance with my
dad for Dylan's birthday
party
  . take ballroom dance,
    with or without my dad
Getting a kitten
  . volunteer at pet shelter?
Coming up with business
ideas
  . work with Matt?
Ice-skating
  . more lessons?
Gingerbread house building
  . gingerbread house
    business?
Geodes
  . rock club? geology club
    after school?

I read over the list and found it very satisfying. (I love making lists! Maybe I should start a list-making club at school!)

As I was tapping my pen against my chin, I heard the doorbell ring downstairs. Looking for a distraction, I popped my head out of my room and listened. There were some voices, and my mom was laughing and saying, "Oh my!" Then she was calling for my dad.

Intrigued, I jogged down the stairs, and right in front of me were two moving men with a piano!

What?

"Mom, do they have the wrong address?" I called.

She turned, laughing. "Nope. It's for you! Read this!" she said, and held out a note to me.

Dear Alexis,

We are so sorry we couldn't make it to your birthday party. I'm sending you my most beloved treasure: my piano. It's all freshly tuned and ready to go. Remember when we used to play for hours? I hope you remember everything I taught you, but even if you don't, I have a feeling you'll pick it up again very quickly. You are so bright and special!

Lots of love,

Granny

"*What?* Is this for real?" I gasped.

My mom nodded as my dad appeared in the hall.

"Wow!" he said. "What's next? A marching band?"

I clapped my hands in excitement and gave a little hop in place. I loved playing the piano with my granny. Whenever we had gone to my grandparents' house—which had been a lot when we were little—my granny and I had played. My mom had bought a little keyboard for me to use at home, but at some point, it broke, and it was never as nice a playing on my grandmother's big, beautiful piano anyway.

I couldn't believe I didn't have playing the piano on my list! I ran back upstairs to add it while the movers got the piano situated in the living room.

Piano playing
. take lessons, practice

There! I wrote "#1" next to it and circled it. I would start with piano. I ran downstairs.

Once they'd set down the bench, I lifted its lid to reveal all the old practice books my granny used to use to teach me to play. Recognizing the one on top, I selected it and sat on the bench to flip through it.

As I flicked past the names of pieces, I was flooded with nostalgia, remembering the times my granny and I would sit together on this bench and play. First, with her playing and my hands on top of hers—almost like how my dad taught me to dance by standing on his feet—then, as I got the hang of it, she "took off the training wheels," and I played alone. She taught me how to read music, and I enjoyed it so much, I occasionally practiced reading it at home.

The piano lessons had been our special cozy time together, and I had loved it. I also always had loved listening to my granny play. She had played in concerts when she was younger and had given piano lessons for years. She had a quiet and peaceful style of playing that I admired. She'd close her eyes and sway a little when she played, and I always thought she looked like the music was taking her away to a magical place.

I settled the book open on a piece called "Arabesque" by a composer named Friedrich Burgmüller. My granny had written in pencil in the margin "Lively, Alexis!" with a little smiley face.

I grinned, placed my hands on the keys, and

began puzzling it out. It was amazing how quickly the tune came back to me—like it had been sitting just inside my fingers for years, waiting to be called out, front and center. My hands had a little trouble finding the proper keys, but I was able to figure it out by ear, and the piece began to sound a little like how it was meant to. I had forgotten how much fun it was to figure out notes and count beats in my head. It was a lot like math, which I love.

Nearly an hour passed, but it felt like only five minutes as I sifted through the old books in the piano bench and selected favorite old songs to try. My mom came in toward the end and stood leaning in the doorway, her arms folded, a smile on her face. When I finished the piece, she clapped.

"When your granny asked if they could give you the piano, I hesitated at first. I said you were so busy with all your activities and friends, and I wasn't sure I wanted a big, hulking piano in my living room. But Granny was confident that you'd go back to it once you had it, and it meant so much to her to hand it down to you."

I folded my hands in my lap and beamed. "It's the best present ever!"

"Should we give her a call to say thanks?" suggested my mom with a big smile.

I nodded.

My mom pulled out her cell phone and dialed Granny. When she picked up, I instantly said, "Thank you! You're the best granny ever! It's Alexis, if you don't know! I love the piano so much!"

I could hear her laughing and telling my grandfather who it was.

"Alexis, sweetheart, I am so happy to hear that! I knew it had to go to just the right person, and that was you."

"Well, I always had so much fun playing it with you, and it's so beautiful. Plus, I've been looking for something . . ." I glanced at my mom, and she smiled and nodded. "Something more to do. Like a new hobby, and this is just the thing."

"Wonderful, darling. You are a born musician. You have the discipline to practice, and you have an organized mind with incredible rhythm and an appreciation for beauty. I know it will give you hours and hours of joy, as it did for me."

"Thank you, Granny! I love you! Have a fun trip!"

"I love you, too, darling. Enjoy!"

After I hung up I spotted a fresh box of our family stationery on my mom's desk. It says "Becker" across the top of the creamy notecards, in blocky navy-blue print.

"Mom! I forgot. I need to write thank-you notes for my presents from my party. Can I use some of the stationery?"

"Of course. That's what it's there for."

I selected a chunk of cards and envelopes and jogged back up to my desk, where I easily wrote thank-yous to Emma, Mia, and Katie for their gifts. It was when I got to Matt that I was stumped. I wrote:

Dear Matt,
Thank you so much for the pen.

And then I got stuck. *It's the best pen ever? It writes so well? I love the feel of it?* It all sounded boring or weird.

You broke my heart by giving me a boring gift, reflecting that I am a boring person who does not inspire feelings of romance in you?

No. I'd better not write that.

I tapped my pen on my chin and reached to open the desk drawer where I'd stowed Matt's pen. I clicked open the lid of its case and looked at it: a wooden pen, lying in blue velvet. The velvet and case seemed like overkill for a silly old pen. I sighed and snapped the lid shut, then I set aside the note for Matt. I needed more inspiration. I'd work on it later.

I had to be at the movie theater by three o'clock, so I was ready by two thirty, of course. My mom was going to drive me on her way to the grocery store. I made a little effort to look nice—I brushed my hair and put on some earrings—because you never know who will be at the mall or the movies, but I still had some time to kill.

I clicked open my e-mail on my computer and saw that the talent show manager had responded to my proposal! He wrote:

Dear Alexis and the Cupcake Club,

Thank you so much for your proposal. It is so well-organized and thought-out. I am very impressed by you young ladies. The school would love to have your cupcake sale at the talent show on Saturday night. We will provide a folding table and two chairs at the theater entrance starting at 6:00 p.m., if you can handle the rest (and I think you can!). I am sorry we can't be of help in staffing the table, but we don't have the extra hands on weekend nights.

If the sale goes well, I would like to speak to the Cupcake Club about working at ten more evening events we have during the school year, including Parents' Night, music recitals, class plays, and PTA meetings.

Please remember no peanuts or tree nuts in the baked goods!

All the best,

Mr. Imbelli

Wow, wow, wow! We just booked ten other jobs at school, assuming everything goes well the night of the talent show! I couldn't wait to tell my friends!

As my mom was dropping me off in front of the mall, I spied the Taylors' silver minivan pulling up behind us. I ran back to meet Emma and tell her the news. As I reached the van, I spotted Matt and Mr. Taylor in the front, with Matt's window rolled down. Yikes. I hadn't seen Matt since my birthday party and the awkward pen-giving. Worse yet, I knew he must have heard about the cheer tryouts and my mortifying fail.

I immediately turned bright red and waved

awkwardly at them as Emma opened the sliding side door to exit.

"Hi, Alexis!" called Mr. Taylor.

Matt waved slightly, with a shy smile. I couldn't stop smiling back, even as butterflies almost flew away with my stomach.

"Hi, Mr. Taylor. Hi, Matt," I said quietly, my voice shaking a little with both love and embarrassment for Matt.

"Have fun at the movies!" Mr. Taylor called as Emma pushed the button for the door to slide closed.

I couldn't think of anything else to say, and certainly nothing to say to Matt. *Think, Becker, think!* But no easy words came to mind as Matt continued to look at me.

"Bye," I said as they pulled away.

Emma stood on the curb and looked at me quizzically. "Is something bad going on with you and Matt?"

I turned to look at her. "What do you mean?"

She knit her eyebrows together. "Are you mad at him or something?"

My jaw dropped. "Me? Mad at Matt? No way! Are you kidding? I just . . ." I couldn't think of how to explain about my weird feelings about his unromantic gift, so I went for the tryouts explanation. "I'm just so mortified that his friend Greg saw my epic fail at the cheerleading tryouts the other day."

Emma looked confused "He did? Well, Matt hasn't mentioned it or anything. What was Greg doing while you were trying out? Was he laughing or something?"

"No, he just looked a little surprised and confused. But I'm sure he told Matt I was awful!"

"Oh, Lex, I'm sure he thought you were good. And I'm sure you *were* good. Or at the very least, you weren't as bad as you think you were! Greg probably didn't even mention it to Matt, because he thought you were just fine. You're too hard on yourself. You're always way better at things than you think."

"Speaking of which, guess who wrote me back?"

I filled Emma in on the Mr. Imbelli e-mail as we rode the escalators up to find Mia and Katie at the theater. When we met up with them, I told them about the ten potential events at school, and we all squealed and jumped up and down. Then I handed each of them the thank-you notes I'd written, and they loved them and hugged me.

After Emma and I picked up our tickets, the

four of us got in line for snacks, and as we stood waiting, Mia cried, "Look! There's Dylan!"

"What?" My heart sank. "What's she doing here? Probably spying on me so she can tell my mom about all the junk food I ate today." I scoffed.

Dylan was kind of decked out—she'd done her hair and makeup, and she had on a pretty top I'd never seen before. She wasn't overdressed, but she looked good, very put-together in a way I will never ever be able to pull off. I was proud of her suddenly, seeing her like that out in public. *That's my big sis,* I thought, before I remembered I currently was mad at her.

"Dylan!" called Katie, but Dylan didn't hear. She was heading over to meet a group of girls standing by the arcade machines. Unlike me, Dylan doesn't have a tight core of three best friends. She has millions of kids she hangs out with, and tons more friends on social media and around town than I do. I know I should try harder to build up my other friendships so I can be more popular, like Dylan, but I don't know how.

"Oh, she's going to meet those girls from the high school, and they're seeing what we're seeing. I was behind them in line," said Katie. "We'll meet up with her inside." Katie turned back to Mia and

Emma as they continued their discussion of how a kid got in trouble in science for dropping the pet snake.

I continued to watch with pride as Dylan approached her group with a smile and then . . . something bad happened. The girls all looked at her and turned their backs on her. Dylan stopped midwalk.

Wait, what?

Then the girls started to laugh, and they scurried away into the ladies' room. Dylan was left standing there, all alone.

My jaw dropped in shock, and I looked quickly at my friends to see if they were interpreting the scene the same way I was. Had Dylan just been ditched?

She stood there, paralyzed, rooted to the spot. I knew how that felt.

"Be right back," I said to my friends. They nodded, still engrossed in their snake conversation. I bolted across the theater to Dylan's side.

"Dilly?" I said. "Hi."

She looked at me as if waking from a dream, a bad one. There were tears in her eyes, but they hadn't fallen and ruined her eye makeup (eye makeup that she had certainly not put on at home, or my mom never would have let her leave the house).

And then, without saying anything, Dylan turned and ran out of the theater.

I chased after her and grabbed her arm just down the hall from the theater. She spun around, crying hard now, her mascara running, and she said, "Leave me alone, Alexis! Just let me be. This is none of your business!" And she ran off again.

I stood there in shock and then slowly, sadly, wandered back to my friends.

CHAPTER 8

Quack

$\mathcal{I}$ did not enjoy the movie.

In fact, I have no idea what the movie was even about. I burned with shame and anger at what had happened to Dylan. When I saw those awful girls from her school file into the theater, I wanted to rip their hair out. How dare they make my sister cry? She was the most fun friend anyone could ask for! I conveniently forgot how annoying and mean Dylan had been last night and how much my parents and friends complimenting her had been bugging me. All I could think of was that she was my sister, and she was in pain, so I was in pain too.

When the movie was over, the only thing I wanted to do was go home.

"Alexis? Did you not like the movie?" asked

Mia. She read my face and looked worried.

"What? No. I mean, it was fine. I'm just . . . I'm really tired. I just want to go home."

My friends exchanged glances.

"Are you okay?" asked Katie, her voice filled with concern.

I took a deep breath. "Yup." I didn't want to add to Dylan's humiliation by explaining what I'd seen.

"But you were so psyched before the show, with the piano news and the cupcake jobs," said Emma, looking at me carefully.

I shrugged. "Yeah, I'm still happy about all that, but I just want to get home. It's been a long day."

"Okay. Want to come sit with us at Jamba Juice until your mom gets here?" asked Mia.

"No, thanks. I'll wait outside," I said.

"Want us to wait with you?" offered Emma.

"Nah, I'm fine. Thanks. I'll talk to you guys tomorrow."

Katie gave me a hug, and I wandered downstairs to wait for my mom, who I'd already texted.

As soon as she pulled up, I hopped in and pulled my seat belt across me, blurting, "What's going on with Dylan?"

My mom took her eyes off the road for a second and looked at me. "Why?" she asked.

"I saw a group of girls be really mean to her at the movies. Like they laughed at her and ditched her. And then she ran away and cried, and I tried to chase her, but she wouldn't let me follow her. I don't know where she went." I thought I might cry myself now.

My mom put her blinker on and carefully pulled to the side of the road and double-parked, her hazard lights clicking out a slow beat. Then she turned to me in her seat and sighed.

"Dad came and got her. Remember how I said that you can never really know what's going on in someone's life? And also how Dad and I had been trying to build Dylan up?"

I nodded.

"Well, she's having a tough time at her school right now. There are some new girls who came in this year who are . . . not very nice girls. They were all friends from Madison"—that's the high school in the rich town next to us—"and they've all come in and completely upended the social structure in Dylan's class."

"Which she was at the top of," I said.

My mom nodded. "And now she seems to be at the bottom." She sighed. "And it's all tied up with cheerleading, because the coach added one of the girls, Jenna somebody, to be Dylan's cocaptain, without telling Dylan. Then Dylan invited the other two to your party, and the Jenna one was upset. . . ."

"Wait, *my* party? Why would anyone care about my party?"

My mom smiled. "It was a great party. I guess the other girl's feelings were hurt, even though it wasn't really Dylan's party. It doesn't even make sense when I say it out loud. I just know that Dylan is hurting right now, and feeling very unsure of herself. That's all. She needs our love and support."

"Wow," I said, shaking my head slowly in wonder. "I just can't believe that about Dylan. She always seems so perfect. Everything always seems to be going so well for her."

My mom laughed gently. "She says the same about you!"

"What? *No way!*"

That was shocking, shocking news, and *duh!* Totally not based in reality. I mean, *seriously*.

"Well, look at what Dylan sees. You get wonderful grades; you have three best friends who would walk over hot coals for you; you have a thriving business, doing something you love; you have an adorable crush who seems to like you back; you're a member of a business club that enriches your life; you're a beautiful dancer. . . ."

"Okay, wait, wait, wait. Yes. That is mostly true, but I'm also boring! I'm not popular, or peppy, or an amazing dresser, or cheer captain, or any of the things Dylan is!"

My mom smiled. "You and Dylan are two very different people, and you're both wonderful just the way you are."

"Hmm. I guess," I said. This was certainly food for thought.

"Okay?" asked my mom.

I nodded, and she slowly pulled back out into the traffic.

"Is Dylan home?" I asked.

"Dad was going to take her to get a bite to eat, but she should be back by now."

"Okay." I knew what I wanted to do.

As soon as I got home, I grabbed an extra note card from the family stationery stash and went up to my desk. I picked up a pen and wrote,

Dear Dylan,
You are the best big sister in the

world, and the coolest person I
know. You are so much fun and
so pretty and generous. You are
an incredible cheerleader, and
you have great fashion sense and
throw amazing parties. All my
friends worship you.

Thank you so much for my
birthday party. It was the best
one I ever had, all thanks to you.

Love, Alexis

I slid the card into its envelope, sealed it, and
wrote "Dylan" on the outside in my best script.
Then I went and slid it under her door.

My mom and I had dinner (since my dad and
Dylan had gone out to eat), and then my parents
and I started to binge-watch a new show. At some
point, Dylan joined us in the family room. My dad
scooted over on the sofa to make room for her, and
she slid in. No one said anything about mean girls
or movie theaters or tears. We just watched the epi-
sodes until we were tired and went to bed.

The next morning I awoke to a text from Emma: Call me.

It was from late the night before. Was she worried about me? Had something happened at the mall after I left? I looked at the time: nine thirty. She was probably up.

I pressed her number and listened to the rings. As I was about to hang up on ring ten, Emma breathlessly answered the phone. "Hi!"

"Hey! What's up? How was the rest of last night?" I asked.

"Oh, kind of lame. We wandered around the food court, and then we ran into Matt with Joe Proctor and George Martinez and had ice cream with them."

I sat up straight in my bed and fluffed the pillows behind me, then sagged into them. "Bummer! I'm so sorry I missed that. I didn't know Matt would be at the mall!"

"It was spontaneous. Joe's dad dropped them off to keep an eye on Joe's little sister and her friends who were alone at the mall for the first time. He paid for their dinner as a thank-you."

"So . . . was it fun?"

"Yeah. Katie and George were flirting up a storm, as usual. They're adorable."

I laughed. "How about you and Joe? And did Mia see anyone cute?"

Emma filled me in, and while I kept hoping she'd mention Matt again, she didn't. Finally, embarrassingly, I had to ask. "So, did . . . Matt ask for me?"

"Oh, yeah. Matt said 'Where's Alexis?' and I said you went home."

"Oh. Was that all?"

"Well, then I asked him if he knew anything about the cheerleading tryouts. Guess what? He didn't know anything! I guess Greg didn't mention it to Matt."

"Wow! That is awesome!"

"I know," agreed Emma. "I just said 'Did anyone say how the cheerleading tryouts went?' And he said no."

"NO?"

"Nope!" Emma laughed. "I knew you'd be happy with that info. That's why I wanted you to call me!"

"Wow, Emma, you are the best! Thank you so much for finding that out for me!"

"Sure. But there's one more thing he did say." Emma's voice grew serious.

"Oh. This doesn't sound good," I said nervously.

"He asked me if you'd mentioned his gift."

Uh-oh.

"He did? Oh."

"He thinks you hated it."

"Oh no!" I bit my lip.

"Well, *did* you?" asked Emma.

"No! No, not at all. I didn't hate it at all!"

"But you didn't like it," Emma said definitively.

"No, it's not that. I *did* like it. It's really nice. It's just. Oh, this is so awkward, especially telling you."

"I don't mind," said Emma. "Go on."

"Well, the thing is, it's a really cool pen. But . . . it's a pen. It's like . . . does he think I'm so boring that he's just inspired to give me a pen or something? It's pretty unromantic. I mean, not that he and I are in some big romance. Ugh. This is so weird, talking to you about your brother like this."

"Hmm. I see what you mean. Well, I didn't see the pen so what do I know? Maybe it has some special romantic significance?" Emma and I both laughed.

"Right!" I said. "Like it's for writing love letters!"

"Yes, maybe it has magical powers so when you write people love notes, they automatically fall in love with you!" she joked. "The pen has a love potion in its ink!"

"I don't know. I really do owe him a thank-you

note. I started it already, but I got stuck."

"'Dear Matt, thanks for the pen. Love, Alexis'?"

"Pretty much." I giggled.

"Well, good luck with that!" said Emma.

I hung up with Emma to find Dylan in my doorway.

"How long have you been standing there?" I asked cautiously.

"Not very long," she said. "Can I come in?"

"Sure."

Dylan walked in and sat in my swivel chair and sighed heavily. "Look, about last night . . ."

"It's okay. You don't have to tell me. Mom explained it all."

"Oh. Okay."

We sat there in silence for a moment, and then she said, "Thanks for your note. That was really nice. I'm sorry I ran away from you at the movie theater."

"That's okay. I was just really worried about you."

Dylan sat up tall. "I can take care of myself."

"I know that. Of course! But I didn't like you being alone when you were feeling so sad."

Dylan sagged back down. "It's been really hard," she said quietly.

"I'm so sorry. You know, you can hang with me and my friends anytime. They all think you're awesome."

Dylan laughed a little. "Thanks. That would be fun. They're really nice girls. We had a good time together planning your party."

"That's what they said too."

There was a pause, and then Dylan said, "You're really lucky, Alexis. Your friends are true-blue."

I smiled sadly. "I know. I wish yours were too."

She shrugged. "I chose badly."

"It's not too late! I'm sure there are lots of other girls in your class who'd like to be your friend. You're so much fun and so smart and pretty and peppy and everything. . . ."

"Humph," said Dylan.

"And you're an amazing cheerleader . . . and party planner!"

Dylan cracked a smile. "Yeah."

We sat for a few seconds in silence, and then I said, "Quack!"

Dylan grinned. She knows the thing our mom always says about acting like a duck and letting things roll off your back. Suddenly, it seemed so silly and funny. Like that all our problems can be made better by uttering this one silly word!

"Quack!" replied Dylan.

"Quack, quack, quack, quack . . . ," I said, laughing now.

"Quack, quack, quack, quack . . ." Dylan was really laughing and flapping her arms like wings.

The more we quacked and flapped, the sillier it seemed, and the more we laughed. Pretty soon, we were hysterical, clutching our sides and rocking back and forth.

You kind of had to be there, but it was great. Our problems weren't solved, but at least we were on the same team again.

CHAPTER 9

Alexis, Alexis, Alexis!

I spent Sunday getting organized for my upcoming history test, a test I was dreading and that was coming up in ten days. Good old practical Alexis, planning ahead, right? But I felt so nervous about it that the only thing I could do was get started. I created a spreadsheet of all the terms I needed to know, then I did another sheet with all the dates, then I did a sheet that had possible essay questions and some bulleted points for the answers. It kind of took all day, but by five o'clock, I had a masterpiece of a study guide.

It was very satisfying work, especially because I knew I had plenty of time before the test so I wouldn't panic come test day.

My mom had made an elaborate meal for

dinner—Dylan's favorite: chicken curry and rice with all the toppings, salad, bread, and key lime pie for dessert. It was amazing, and it put us all in a great mood. We cleaned up together to music that Dylan played from her speaker, and my dad got so into the music that he ended up starting a little dance-off competition, to see who had the best moves!

After dinner we played cards—this knocking game we always play if we go on a trip—and Dylan won. I couldn't tell if my parents let her win, but I didn't mind even if they did. I knew they were trying to give her a boost, and I was all for it.

My family went to sleep that night feeling very happy and peaceful with one another, and most importantly, very connected. We knew that we had one another's backs, and it was a great feeling to be starting the week like that. I hoped things would get better for Dylan at school, but at least she knew she had a strong home base to come back to.

That week, the piano became my obsession. I scheduled all my homework so that I could reward myself with playing time, and I found myself quickly getting better at the familiar old pieces and hungering for new challenges. I even stopped by our school library to take out a couple of extra piano books to see if I could teach myself some new songs.

I kept finding my dad leaning in the living room doorway, listening to me play with a small smile. When I asked him why he was standing there, he said it reminded him of being a kid and listening to his own mom play. After hearing that I e-mailed my grandma to see if there were some pieces she could recommend that she used to play. I thought maybe I'd learn them and surprise my dad one day.

Dylan got annoyed with me on Tuesday. We were at dinner, and my parents were asking about our days. Dylan said hers was fine, but she didn't want to discuss it. I saw my parents exchange a glance, and I must have been looking at Dylan with a sad expression because she snapped at me.

"I don't need your pity, Alexis. I'm not a total loser, you know!" she said, scowling.

"Sor-*ry*!" I said. "Pardon me for feeling sympathetic!"

My dad tried to change the subject. "Alexis, your playing is coming along beautifully! I love hearing you on the piano when I come home from work."

"Thanks, I—"

Dylan interrupted. "Alexis, Alexis, Alexis," she singsonged. "Alexis is so perfect. She does everything so well. She's our favorite daughter. . . ."

Wait, *what*?

"That's enough, Dylan. If you can't be kind, you may be excused. Please apologize to Alexis either way," said my dad.

Dylan didn't want to leave the table. She cast her eyes down and mumbled an apology, and we all continued to eat as if nothing had happened.

But inside, I was reeling from shock! Had Dylan just said about me exactly what I'd been saying about her for the past few weeks? It was impossible to believe!

That night I was in bed studying for history again when my mom came into my room to say good night. I put down my study guide and said, "I guess it's not getting any better for Dylan at school this week, is it?"

My mom shook her head sadly and sighed. "I might have to go in to have a chat with the teachers and see what can be done."

"Wow. Sorry." I'd dealt with my fair share of mean girls before—including Olivia Allen, the worst of all—so I kind of knew how that felt. "I wish there was something I could do to help make her feel better."

"That's very generous, honey. I'm sure she'd appreciate that. Thank you."

As I went to sleep I had a couple of really great ideas for what I could do to cheer up Dylan. I sat up and scribbled them down and then slept like a baby until my alarm went off.

At lunch the next day, I came clean with the Cupcakers and told them what was going on with Dylan. I thought it might be disloyal of me to do so, but I also had to enlist their help in cheering her up. (Ha-ha, get it? Cheering?)

"I'm going to ask her to help us with a couple of Cupcake Club things and see if it makes her feel better. So that's why I was wondering if I could host the Cupcake Club meeting again this week at my house, please?"

"You mean now you *want* us to hang out with Dylan?" asked Mia

I sighed. "Uh-huh, yup. Sorry for all the confusion."

"Poor Dylan," said Katie.

"I know," I agreed.

"We're in. Whatever you want," offered Mia.

"Thanks."

That night I asked Dylan if she would help me create a playlist for our Cupcake Club meetings. I said we needed some energizing music and something to inspire our creativity a little—we were kind of in a rut. Even though I'd made it up, as I said it, I knew it was true. I invited her to join us on Friday.

Dylan looked at me skeptically, as if she knew I was asking her just to be nice.

I waited.

Then after a few seconds she said, "Okay, if I'm home, I'll stop by."

That was the best I could hope for.

On Friday my friends all came over. Katie and Emma were chattering away about the piece Emma was playing with her teacher at the talent show the next day, and I was just hoping my little Operation Cheer Up Dylan would work.

We got home and prepared a snack, and while we ate, I read aloud from our ledger, which is where we keep track of our profits and spending. We'd been a little flat lately, and we needed some new ideas, more events, and more creativity.

"It's time to take it up a notch!" I announced.

As if on cue Dylan came in the back door and shut it hard. I cocked my head, trying to decide if that was a firm shut or a door slam. I'd know soon enough.

Dylan walked into the kitchen.

"Hey, Dylan!" said my friends, truly happy to see her.

"Want a snack?" offered Katie. She always concocted some delicious thing out of nothing—like today it was pizza English muffins with a little tomato sauce she had whipped up with ingredients from the cabinet and topped with some grated mozzarella and Parmesan. They were insanely good!

Dylan looked as if she was going to decline, but then she saw the mini pizzas on the platter and said yes. She selected one, put it on a paper towel, and sat down to join us.

This was going well so far!

"Girls, I asked Dylan if she might have time to create a playlist for us for our meetings and baking sessions. I think it will help pump us up a little."

"Ooh, good idea!" said Mia, looking expectantly at Dylan.

Dylan had her mouth full, but she nodded. "Amazing pizzas, Katie," she said, and Katie beamed. Dylan wiped her fingers on the paper towel and pulled out her phone. "I actually did a little brainstorming during lunch today. . . ."

I didn't want to think about why she might have had the time to brainstorm on her phone during lunch, since it could only mean one thing: She'd eaten alone. I just congratulated myself that step one of my cheer-up plan had worked. She was getting involved with us and had something else to think about besides the mean girls.

"I think we should start with some really upbeat songs to get you moving around and get your heart rates up, almost like a warm-up." She listed a few Top 40–type pop songs from the past few years that were all fun. "Then we get a little groovier. . . ." Dylan rattled off ten songs I'd never heard of, but the other girls had and they looked psyched.

"Those are really good," said Emma, who knows more about popular music than I do. She nodded in approval.

"And then another peppy interlude to keep your energy up, and that you can sing along to, to inspire you and raise your endorphins, those feel-good chemicals in your body." Dylan fired off five more songs. "And that should do it."

She put her phone back down and picked up her pizza.

"Those are really good ideas," said Katie. Then she turned to me. "Alexis, I love the baking session playlist concept!"

I smiled. "Thanks. I was also thinking, Dylan, if

your schedule has the time for it, is there any way you could please do our hair and makeup before the talent show bake sale tomorrow? That way we'll all look really professional, especially Emma, who has to perform. If it works out, you could do it for the other events we're doing at school too."

"Yes, please!" Emma said in relief. "I'm going to be too nervous and distracted to do it myself, and I'd love your help. Oh, Dylan, please say yes!"

I shot Emma a warning look, as if to say, *Don't overdo it*. She caught my eye and nodded slightly.

"What time is it tomorrow?" asked Dylan through a mouthful of pizza.

"The doors open at six, but we need to be there at five thirty to set up."

Dylan thought for a minute, and I held my breath. Finally, "I'm free before then," she agreed.

"Awesome. Thank you so much! We were planning to meet here at three o'clock to do the frosting and chop the toppings. Should we come a little earlier?" asked Katie.

"Mmm, I think I can be here by two o'clock," said Dylan.

I had one more thing up my sleeve.

"Also, Dylan, I have another concept. Katie had actually mentioned this before, but I was thinking maybe you'd like to come on board with the Cupcake Club as our party-planning-services coordinator."

I smiled and sat back in my seat proudly and looked around the table, but my friends were all looking at me in shock. That was not the reaction I was expecting.

"What?" I asked.

They looked at one another, and Emma cleared her throat, but Dylan said flatly, "No. Thanks. That's just not an interest of mine."

"But you're so good at it!" I said, leaning forward in my chair.

My friends still had anxious looks on their faces, but now they were looking between me and Dylan, as if we were having a ping-pong match.

"Alexis, nothing personal, but planning and organizing and all that—I don't really enjoy it. I mean, if it's for a person I know, like your birthday party, then yes, obviously. But as, like, a job? No, thanks."

Emma let out a huge sigh of what seemed to be relief.

"Anyway, I'm too busy now."

Um, what?

"With school?" I asked, cringing as I said it. I

knew Dylan would now be mad at me for letting on that her social life wasn't so great.

"No, not with school," she said witheringly. "I've been brought on as a consultant to the middle school cheerleading program."

"Whaaaaat?" My jaw dropped in surprise.

Dylan nodded. "That Ceci girl texted and said that Ms. Adorante, the faculty adviser, suggested I help out a couple of days a week as, like, a junior coach." She shrugged. "So I said yes."

I didn't want to overreact with joy, but this was the best thing I'd heard in weeks! It would get Dylan away from the mean girls, get her doing something she loved, and with someone as nice as Ceci—well, it was a win-win! But I played it cool.

"Okay, I get it. That's totally fine. Maybe you'd just be available for advice sometimes, like party planning brainstorming."

"If I'm free," said Dylan. She stood and wiped the crumbs from where she'd been sitting. "And, Alexis, I'm on to your whole 'Let's be nice to Dylan to cheer her up' plan. I appreciate it, but I can take care of myself. I'll e-mail you the playlist link when I get upstairs. See you tomorrow at two o'clock. Thanks for the pizza, Katie." And she left.

We all waited until we heard her door close

upstairs, and then everyone spoke at once.

"Oh thank goodness for Ceci Shanahan," I said first.

"Alexis, what were you thinking?" said Emma.

"She sure got you, Alexis!" said Katie, laughing.

"I'm just psyched for Dylan to do my makeup!" crowed Mia.

We all laughed.

"Okay, I am sorry. I went too far. I just was surprised she kept saying yes, and that party planner thing was, like, Plan Z in case she said no to the other things."

"Alexis, you have to clear stuff like that with us first," Emma said quietly but firmly. "I mean, the playlist and the makeup and hair . . . Those are one-offs. But when you're talking about basically adding a new member to our club, someone we'll have to split profits with and whatever, you can't just go ahead willy-nilly like that."

I hung my head. "I'm sorry. You're right. I shouldn't have done that without discussing it with you first."

"Well, she said no, so it's not an issue," said Katie, who is always our peacemaker.

"I think Dylan is on the mend," I said. "She seems more back to her usual self."

"I hope so," said Mia. "Now let's get baking!"

Emma picked up her phone to clear off the table as a workspace, and then she cried, "Oh no!" with such alarm that we all gasped. *"What?"*

CHAPTER 10

Three Cheers for Me

$\mathcal{M}$y music teacher's daughter broke her ankle playing soccer at her college, and my teacher has to fly there to be with her for surgery!"

"Oh no! The poor thing!" said Katie.

"No, poor *me*! I know it's awful and I shouldn't feel sorry for myself, but now she won't be here to play the piano with me in our duet at the talent show. And it's tomorrow!" Emma sank down into a chair and put her face in her hands.

"Oh, Emma!" said Mia, sitting down next to her and patting her back.

"Can you play something else?" asked Katie.

"I've been practicing this piece for weeks," said Emma. "It's too late."

We all sat there grimly for a minute.

Then reluctantly, I said, "How hard is the piano part?"

Emma took her hands off her face and sighed. "Not too bad. It's really just chords, set to a certain rhythm. The flute part that I play is the complicated part: the melody."

I pressed my lips together and took a deep breath. "Do you want me to try to play it with you?"

Emma looked at me. "You? I mean, thanks, but . . . can you really play?"

I shrugged. "I can play better than . . . an empty chair!"

Emma looked confused, and then she laughed. "You mean you're better than no one?"

I shrugged and smiled. "What you see is what you get!"

Katie stood up. "Mia and I are going to make the cupcakes now. You girls go in the living room and get started on the duet."

"Let me print out the sheet music, and I'll get my flute," said Emma, popping over to our family computer on the desk in the corner of the kitchen.

Minutes later, the two of us were sitting on the piano bench together in the living room, and Emma was showing me what to do.

It wasn't easy, but it wasn't hard, if you know what I mean. Emma was scribbling notes in the margins of the music to dumb it down a little for me, and I was picking it up as I went along.

"Okay, let's try it together." Emma picked up her flute and began to play a beautiful melody. I started listening to her and forgot to move my hands over the piano keys, so she stopped playing.

"Um, Alexis?" she asked.

"Right! Sorry! It just sounds so good!"

We started up again and inched our way through the piece, stopping and starting and tweaking it. Then we did it again and again. Soon, we were flowing along, and the smell of baking cupcakes wafted through the air.

"Good old Katie and Mia," I said, sniffing.

"Good old Alexis, you mean. Thank you so much for being willing to help me."

"Let's just keep practicing until we get it right," I said.

"Okay," agreed Emma. "But you can't spend all of tonight and all day tomorrow on this. What about studying for the history test?"

"Please," I said. "I've been studying for that thing for ages!"

"Oh, Lex. You're so organized!" Emma laughed.

"That's just one of the things that makes you such a great friend!"

"So that was a bit of an epic Cupcake Club session," I said, two hours later.

There were racks of cupcakes cooling all over our kitchen. My fingers were sore from the piano practice; Katie and Mia both had flour in their hair; and we still had to get to the grocery store to buy some toppings for tomorrow. Then there was the frosting to make and use, and dropping off Mona's minis in the morning, then dressing and primping, and all the practice that Emma and I could fit in in time for the talent show. Plus, they all needed to study for the history test.

"Guess what? Alexis already studied for the history exam," said Emma.

"Of course she did!" Mia said with a laugh.

"That's our girl!" Katie giggled.

"Well, a stitch in time saves nine, that's what I always say. And a good thing I did it in advance, anyway, or I wouldn't have time to practice for the talent show tomorrow."

"Guys, guess what? She's really good on the piano too!" said Emma.

"I'm not surprised," said Mia, hugging my neck.

"Please, this is going to my head!" I joked.

"You deserve all the compliments in the world!" said Katie, just as Dylan walked into the room.

I braced myself for some snarky Dylan comment, but she just smiled and nodded.

"She does," said Dylan.

I waited for the zinger, but one didn't come. Was that it? Dylan refilled her water bottle from the cooler and left the room, and I exhaled a breath I hadn't realized I was holding.

"That was pretty nice, right?" Emma said quietly.

"Really unexpected," I agreed in wonder. "And nice."

Everyone needed to go home and get on with their lives. I was going to take a study break now (meaning, a break from piano, to study!), and then I'd practice some more piano before the night was over. I agreed to go to the store with my dad later for the topping supplies. Katie was going to come first thing tomorrow to pick up Mona's minis for delivery. Emma would come back in the morning for another duet practice session, and then the other girls would come over to help with frosting. We'd break for lunch and then regroup to get dressed and have our hair and makeup done.

After everyone left I went upstairs to my desk to

just catch my breath for a minute. I spied my half-written note for Matt and felt bad. It was overdue, and Emma had implied that he felt weird about the gift. Sighing, I opened my desk drawer and pulled out the pen box and opened it, hoping for some inspiration for my note. I went to lift out the pen from its box, but I fumbled, and it dropped on my rug. As I bent to pick it up, I saw something glinting on the side of the barrel, something golden. I lifted the pen and saw an inscription in gold letters: $M + A$

Wow! Matt plus Alexis? It had to be! How could I be so silly? This was an amazing present! Matt had basically put it in writing that he liked me! Plus, let's face it, what my mom had said was true! I didn't want some frivolous junk—some random gift that said my closest friends (or crushes!) didn't even know me. This was a thoughtful gift, with a sprinkle of romance on top, and it was just perfect for me!

I reached over and without even struggling, finished the note to Matt, thanking him profusely for such a wonderful, beautiful, useful pen, and thanking him for knowing me so well.

I signed it just A. I figured he'd know that meant I'd seen the inscription and liked it. I slid the card into the envelope, wrote "M" on the outside, and sealed it up. I'd have my dad swing by the Taylors' house so I could drop it through their mail slot on the way to the grocery store tonight. Now that I'd seen the real romantic nature of Matt's gift, I didn't want to delay my acknowledgment even one minute longer!

To say the next day was a frenzy would be an understatement. I woke up at the crack of dawn to make the vanilla icing and frost Mona's minis, then pack them up. Katie and Katie's mom came by at nine to get them, and Emma arrived not long after they left to start practicing. We had to make the most of the day.

Fortified with my dad's buckwheat pancakes, we practiced and practiced until we hit a wall. As we stopped after our tenth time in a row, there was a slow clap from the hall. It was Dylan, standing in the doorway.

"You guys sound great," she said. "Totally in sync and smooth, just like best friends should."

I squinted, trying to decide if she was being sarcastic or serious, but she smiled. "I mean it, Alexis. You don't have to look so suspicious."

"Thanks," said Emma. "Are you coming to the

talent show tonight?" she asked. "I hope so!"

"I wish I could," said Dylan. "I know you guys will be amazing. It's just . . . I have a meeting for the middle school cheerleading. Actually, middle and high school."

I raised my eyebrows in surprise. "Are you . . . happy about the high school part? I wasn't sure . . ."

Dylan nodded. "The new girl, Jenna, who our coach promoted to be my cocaptain? She's actually pretty nice. So, I invited her to come meet Ceci with me and see if we could maybe do some combined practices this year. Kind of a mentoring thing, but kind of also for brainstorming. Sometimes the younger girls have fresh ideas."

I smiled. "That's great, Dylan. What a good idea."

"Thanks. Well, I'm going to see if there are any pancakes left. See you girls later for the makeup and all."

She left, and Emma and I looked at each other and smiled.

"I'm proud Dylan," she said.

"Me too."

Everyone showed up with wet hair, as instructed by Dylan, and she lined us up in her room and blew out our hair, one by one. Then she told us to put on our outfits, and she'd do our makeup. She was supernice to us all.

I hurried to grab my new velvet dress she'd given me. It was just the perfect thing to wear tonight. I was so psyched.

"Is . . . um, Matt coming tonight?" I asked Emma, gently pulling the dress over my head. I couldn't wait and wonder anymore.

"Yup," said Emma. "My whole family's coming!"

I felt the butterflies take flight in my stomach, and my hands grew cold. Matt would see me perform tonight.

Emma shot me a look. "Don't get all nervous. This time you're prepared."

"I know, I know. Deep breaths. Yoga poses!" I said, thinking of Ceci's little brother.

"Hey, everyone, look what I brought!" said Katie. "Feather tattoos from Lit Beauty!"

We put them on, in the same spot on our arms, and we held them out to admire, all in a row.

"Birds of a feather, stick together!" I said.

"Quack!" Dylan said as she entered the room with her makeup kit. And we cracked up.

The talent show bake sale was a huge hit, and Mr. Imbelli was thrilled. We sold so many cupcakes before the show even started that he asked us to bring even more next time, which meant there would be a next time for sure—or ten next times!

It was fun seeing everyone come in for the show, including teachers, all dressed up, and the whole Taylor family, and my family. Matt looked so handsome in a pale blue button-down shirt that matched his eyes.

"Thanks for the note," he said with a huge grin.

I blushed furiously and said, "Thanks for the pen," and we both laughed.

"You look great," Matt said.

"So do you," I said, smiling so hard I thought my cheeks would fall off.

Emma's little brother, Jake, looked back and forth between the both of us and said, "You two are weirdos," which made us crack up even more. I had a smile on my face for the whole night after that.

When it came time to go in for the show, we put up a little sign on our table that said THE CUPCAKE CLUB IS CLOSED UNTIL INTERMISSION, then Mia and Katie ran to take their seats, and Emma and I scooted around backstage.

Behind the curtain, Emma and I hugged tightly until our names were called. Then we took deep breaths and smiled, and we walked out onto the stage holding hands. Beyond the bright lights, I could make out my parents, Mia, Katie, and the Taylors, all sitting together in the same row, smiling at us. Instead of making me feel nervous, it made me feel brave. Our families and friends had our backs.

Off to the side, someone was waving at me, and it caught my eye. It was Dylan, sitting with Ceci and a redheaded girl I didn't recognize, who must've been Jenna. I couldn't believe they came. Dylan gave me a thumbs-up, and I smiled at them and sat down at the piano to play.

Emma and I made eye contact as she settled in front of her music stand and lifted the flute to her lips. Then, just as we'd practiced, she nodded once, and we began.

It went perfectly! We played like we'd been playing together for years, and the billowing sound filled the theater and washed over us all, filling us with happiness. Before I knew it, it was over, and everyone was cheering and giving us a standing ovation! We hadn't messed up once.

We left the stage but ran back out for a curtain call, and suddenly, Matt was coming up the steps at the edge of the stage, with big bouquets of roses for each of us. He gave Emma a hug as she accepted the roses, and then he turned to me and gave me mine. He leaned in and gave me a kiss, right on my cheek, and I nearly fainted away with happiness. He smiled as he pulled back, and I grinned so hard it hurt.

Later, we celebrated in the lobby with more cupcakes. (We sold out! I couldn't believe it! After all my careful planning!) Matt and I chatted the whole time. It was one of the best nights of my life.

We were some of the last people to leave, and as Emma and I lugged our cupcake carriers to my car, I stopped in the parking lot.

"Em, thanks so much for taking a chance on me," I said. "That was an amazing night, and I never would have been a part of it if it weren't for you."

Emma laughed. "It's me who needs to be thanking you! You're the best friend a girl could ever have! You're organized and generous and persistent. I can't believe you learned that whole song just to help me! Plus organizing the cupcake sale and all the hair and makeup and whatever. You're amazing!" She put down her cupcake carriers and flung her arms around me. "Thank you so much, Lexi!"

I hugged her back, sort of, since my cupcake carriers were awkwardly still in my hands. "No problemo," I said. "I guess that's just who I am." I tried to act as if it was no big deal, but inside I felt pretty great.

That night, after the show, I opened an e-mail from my grandma. It had sheet music attached, so I printed it out, then snuck off to the living room to give it a try. What the heck? I was on a roll!

A couple of minutes later, I heard someone at the door. It was my dad, and he had tears in his eyes.

"Oh, Alexis, I can't tell you how good it makes me feel to hear that piece again! It was my favorite when I was a boy."

I grinned and kept plugging away at it.

When I looked up again, my mom was standing with him in the doorway, her arm around his waist.

"We're so proud of you, Alexis. You are a wonderful kid, a great sister, and friend," she said.

I put my hands in my lap and smiled. "I'm just trying to be the best Alexis I can be."

"That's all we'd ever hope for you," said my mom.

"Me too," I agreed. "Me too."

Here's a small taste
of the very first book in the

series written by Coco Simon:

SUNDAY
SUNDAES

PLOT TWIST

A hot August wind lifted my brown hair and cooled the back of my neck as I waited for the bus to take me to my new school. I hoped I was standing in the right spot. I hoped I was wearing the right thing. I wished I were anywhere else.

My toes curled in my new shoes as I reached into my messenger bag and ran my thumb along the worn spine of my favorite book. I'd packed *Anne of Green Gables* as a good-luck charm for my first day at my new school. The heroine, Anne Shirley, had always cracked me up and given me courage. To me, having a book around was like having an old friend for company. And, boy, did I need a friend right about now.

Ten days before, I'd returned from summer

camp to find my home life completely rearranged. It hadn't been obvious at first, which was almost worse. The changes had come out in drips, and then all at once, leaving me standing in a puddle in the end.

My mom and dad picked me up after seven glorious weeks of camp up north, where the temperature is cool and the air is sweet and fresh. I was excited to get home, but as soon as I arrived, I missed camp. Camp was fun, and freedom, and not really worrying about anything. There was no homework, no parents, and no little brothers changing the ringtone on your phone so that it plays only fart noises. At camp this year I swam the mile for the first time, and all my camp besties were there. My parents wrote often: cheerful e-mails, mostly about my eight-year-old brother, Tanner, and the funny things he was doing. When they visited on Parents' Weekend, I was never really alone with them, so the conversation was light and breezy, just like the weather.

The ride home was normal at first, but I noticed my parents exchanging glances a couple of times, almost like they were nervous. They looked different too. My dad seemed more muscular and was tan, and my mom had let her hair—dark brown and wavy, like mine—grow longer, and it made her look younger. The minute I got home, I grabbed my sweet cat, Diana (named after Anne Shirley's best friend, naturally), and scrambled into my room. Sharing a bunkhouse with eleven other girls for a summer was great, but I was really glad to be back in my own quiet room. I texted **SHE'S BAAAACK!** to my best friends, Tamiko Sato and Sierra Perez, and then took a really long, hot shower.

It wasn't until dinnertime that things officially got weird.

"You must've really missed me," I said as I sat down at the kitchen table. They'd made all of my favorites: meat lasagna, garlic bread, and green salad with Italian dressing and cracked pepper. It was the meal we always had the night before I left for camp and the night I got back. My mouth started watering.

I grinned as I put my napkin onto my lap.

"We *did* miss you, Allie!" said my mom brightly.

"They talked about you all the time," said Tanner, rolling his eyes and talking with his mouth full of garlic bread, his dinner napkin still sitting prominently on the table.

"Napkin on lapkin!" I scolded him.

"Boys don't use napkins. That's what sleeves are

for," said Tanner, smearing his buttery chin across the shoulder of his T-shirt.

"Gross!" Coming out of the all-girl bubble of camp, I had forgotten the rougher parts of the boy world. I looked to my parents to reprimand him, but they both seemed lost in thought. "Mom? Dad? Hello? Are you okay with this?" I asked, looking to both of them for backup.

"Hmm? Oh, Tanner, don't be disgusting. Use a napkin," said my mom, but without much feeling behind it.

He smirked at me, and when she looked away, he quickly wiped his chin on his sleeve again. It was like all the rules had flown out the window since I'd been gone!

My dad cleared his throat in the way he usually did when he was nervous, like when he had to practice for a big sales presentation. I looked up at him; he was looking at my mom with his eyebrows raised. His bright blue eyes—identical to mine— were *definitely* nervous.

"What's up?" I asked, the hair on my neck prickling a little. When there's tension around, or sadness, I can always feel it. It's not like I'm psychic or anything. I can just feel people's feelings coming off them in waves. Maybe my parents' fighting as I was growing up had made me sensitive to stuff, or maybe it was from reading so many books and feeling the characters' feelings along with them. Whatever it was, my mom said I had a lot of empathy. And right now my empathy meter was registering *high alert.*

My mom swallowed hard and put on a sunny smile that was a little too bright. Now I was really suspicious. I glanced at Tanner, but he was busy dragging a slab of garlic bread through the sauce from his second helping of lasagna.

"Allie, there's something Dad and I would like to tell you. We've made some new plans, and we're pretty excited about them."

I looked back and forth between the two of them. What she was saying didn't match up with the anxious expressions on their faces.

"They're getting divorced," said Tanner through a mouthful of lasagna and bread.

"What?" I said, shocked, but also . . . kind of not. I felt a huge sinking in my stomach, and tears pricked my eyes. I knew there had been more fighting than usual before I'd left for camp, but I hadn't really seen this coming. Or maybe I had; it was like divorce had been there for a while, just slightly to the side of everything, riding shotgun all along. Automatically my brain raced through the list of

book characters whose parents were divorced: Mia in the Cupcake Diaries, Leigh Botts in *Dear Mr. Henshaw*, Karen Newman in *It's Not the End of the World*. . . .

My mother sighed in exasperation at Tanner.

"Wait, Tanner knew this whole time and I didn't?" I asked.

"Sweetheart," said my dad, looking at me kindly. "This has been happening this summer, and since Tanner was home with us, he found out about it first." Tanner smirked at me, but Dad gave him a look. "I know this is hard, but it's actually really happy news for me and your mom. We love each other very much and will stay close as a family."

"We're just tired of all the arguing. And we're sure you two are too. We feel that if we live apart, we'll be happier. All of us."

My mind raced with questions, but all that came out was, "What about me and Tanner? And Diana? Where are we going to live?"

"Well, I found a great apartment right next to the playground," said my dad, suddenly looking happy for real. "You know that new converted factory building over in Maple Grove, with the rooftop pool that we always talk about when we pass by?"

"And I've found a really great little vintage

house in Bayville. And you won't believe it, but it's right near the beach!"

I stared at them.

Mom swallowed hard and kept talking. "It's just been totally redone, and the room that will be yours has built-in bookcases all around it and a window seat," she said.

"And it has a hot tub," added my dad.

"Right," laughed my mom. "And there are plantings in the flower beds around the house, so we can have fresh flowers all spring, summer, and fall!" My mom loved flowers, but my dad grew up doing so much yard work for his parents that he refused to ever let her plant anything here. The house did sound nice, but then something occurred to me.

"Wait, Bayville and Maple Grove? So what about school?" Bayville was ten minutes away!

"Well." My parents shared a pleased look as my mom spoke. "Since my new house is in Bayville, you qualify for seventh grade at the Vista Green School! It's the top-rated school in the district, and it's gorgeous! Everything was newly built just last year. Tan will go to MacBride Elementary."

"Isn't that great?" said my dad.

"Um, *what*? We're changing *schools*?" The lasagna was growing cold on my plate, but how could I eat?

I looked at Tanner to see how he was reacting to all this news, but he was nearly finished with his second helping of lasagna and showed no sign of stopping. The shoulder of his T-shirt now had red sauce stains smeared across it. I looked back at my mom.

"Yes, sweetheart. I know it will be a big transition at first. Everything is going to be new for us all! A fresh start!" said my mom enthusiastically.

Divorce. Moving. A new school.

"Is there any *more* news?" I asked, picking at a crispy corner of my garlic bread.

"Actually," my mom began, looking to my dad, "I have some really great news. Dad and I decided it probably wasn't a good idea for me to go on being the chief financial officer of his company. So I've rented a space in our new neighborhood, and . . . I'm opening an ice cream store, just like I've always dreamed! Ta-da!" She threw her arms wide and grinned.

My jaw dropped as I lifted my head in surprise. "Really?" My mom made the best—I mean the absolute *best*—homemade ice cream in the world. She made a really thick, creamy ice cream base, and then she was willing to throw in anything for flavor: lemon and blueberries, crumbled coffee cake, crushed candy canes, you name it. She was known for her ice cream. I mean, people came to our house and actually asked if she had any in the freezer.

My mom was nodding vigorously, the smile huge on her face. She looked happier and younger than I'd seen her in years. And my dad looked happier than he had in a long time.

"And you two can be the taste testers!" said my mom.

"Yessss!" said Tanner, pumping his fist out and back against his chest. "And our friends, too?" he asked.

"Yes. All of your friends can test flavors too," said my mom.

"Okay, wait." I couldn't take this all in at once. It felt like someone had removed my life and replaced it with a completely new version.

Who were these people? What was my family? *Who was I?*

"Eat your dinner, honey," urged my dad. "It's your favorite. There's plenty of time to talk through all of this."

My eyes suddenly brimmed with tears; I just couldn't help it. Even if—and this was a big "if" for me—this would be a good move for our family, there was still a new house and a new *school*. What about my friends? What about Book Fest, the reading celebration at my school that I helped organize and was set to run this year?

I wiped my eyes with my sleeve. "What about Book Fest?" I said meekly.

My mom stood and came around to hug me. "Oh, Allie, I'm sure they'll still let you come."

I pulled away. "Come? I *run* it! Who's going to run it now? And what will I do instead?"

I scraped my chair away from the table, pulled away from my mom, and raced to my room. Diana was curled up on my bed, and she jumped when I closed the door hard behind me. (It wasn't a slam, but almost.) I grabbed Diana, flopped onto the bed, and had a good cry. Certainly Anne Shirley would have thrown herself onto her bed and cried, at least at first. But what would Hermione Granger have done? Violet Baudelaire? Katniss Everdeen? My favorite characters encountered a lot of troubles, but they usually got through them okay, and it wasn't by lying around crying about them. I sniffed and reached for a tissue, and slid up against my head-board into a sitting position so that I could have a good think, like a plot analysis.

My parents had been unhappy for a long time. I kind of knew that. I mean, I guess we were all unhappy because Mom and Dad fought a lot.

They both worked hard at their jobs, and I knew they were tired, so I always thought a lot of it was just crankiness. Plus Mom was the business manager and my dad ran the marketing group at their company, so I figured since they worked together all day, they just got on each other's nerves after work. But if I really thought about it, I realized that they were like that on the weekends, and even on holidays and vacations. They snapped at each other. They rolled their eyes. And sometimes one of them stomped out of the room. And the more I thought about it, I realized they hadn't spent a lot of time together over the past year. Either Mom would be taking me to soccer and Dad would be staying home with Tanner, or Dad would be doing carpool and errands while Mom went with Tanner to his music lessons. We always ate dinner together, but starting last winter and right up to when I'd left for camp, there had been a lot of pretty quiet meals, with each of us lost in our own thoughts. Mom would talk to me or to Tanner, and Dad would always ask about our days, but they never actually spoke to each other.

I squeezed my eyes shut and tried to think of the last time we'd all been happy together. The night before I left for camp, maybe? We had my favorite dinner, and Dad was teasing that it would be the last great meal before I ate camp food for the summer. Mom joked that we should sneak some lasagna into my shoes, which Tanner thought was a really good idea. Dad ran and picked up one of my sneakers, and Mom pretended to spoon some in. We were being silly and laughing, and I felt warm and snug and cozy. I loved camp and couldn't wait to go every year, but I remembered thinking right then that I'd miss being at the table with my family around me.

Later that night, though, I heard Mom and Dad fighting about something in their room, like they seemed to do almost every night. Then for seven weeks I went to sleep hearing crickets and giggles instead of angry whispers, along with a few warnings of "Girls, it's time to go to bed!" from my counselors.

Now I heard whispers from Mom and Dad on the other side of the door. They weren't angry, but they didn't sound happy, either. Then I heard the whispers fade as they went downstairs.

I guess I fell asleep, because when I woke up, Dad was sitting on my bed and Mom was standing next to him, looking worried. The lights were out, but my room was bright from the moon.

"Allie," Dad said gently. "You need to brush your teeth and get ready for bed."

"Do you want to talk about anything?" Mom asked as I sat up.

Suddenly I was really annoyed. "Oh, you mean like how you decided to get a divorce and not tell me? Or sell our house and not tell me? Or that I would need to move schools and totally start over again? Nope, nothing to discuss at all." I crossed my arms over my chest.

"Allie," Mom said, and her voice broke. I could tell she was upset, but I didn't care. "We are divorcing because we think it will make us happier. All of us."

"Speak for yourself," I said. I knew I was being mean, and on any usual day one of them would tell me to watch my tone.

"It is going to be hard," said Dad slowly. "It's going to be an adjustment, and it's going to take a lot of patience from all of us. We are not sugarcoating that part. But it's going to be better. You and Tanner mean everything to us, and Mom and I are going to do what will make you happiest. This separation will make us stronger as a family. Things will be better, and we need you to believe that."

"And what if I don't?" I said. I knew I was on thin ice. Even I could tell that I sounded a little bratty. "What will make me happiest is to stay in this house and go to the same school with my friends and . . ." I thought about it for a second. "Wait, if I'm moving to Bayville, when will I ever see Dad?"

"A lot still needs to be worked out," said Mom. "For now you and Tanner and Diana will live with me at the house in Bayville during the week. Dad will come over every Wednesday, and every other weekend you'll be at Dad's apartment in Maple Grove."

I looked at Dad. "So every other week I'll only see you on Wednesdays?" I felt my eyes filling with tears again.

"We can work things out, Allie," said Dad quickly. "I am still here and I am still your dad and I will always be around."

"I promise you, Allie, we're going to do everything we can to make this better for all of us," Mom said. I couldn't see her face clearly, but I could see that she was trying hard not to cry.

Dad reached over and gave Mom's arm a little squeeze. I sat there looking at them, not being able to remember the last time I'd seen Mom give Dad a kiss hello, or Dad hug Mom. Now here they were, but even that didn't seem right.

"I'm not brushing my teeth," I said. I don't really know why I said that. I guess I just wanted to feel like I was still in control of something, anything. Then I turned away from them and pulled up the covers. All I wanted to do was go to sleep, because I was really hoping I would wake up and this would all be a bad dream.

I woke up and blinked a few times, remembering that I was back in my room at home and not still at camp. Well, home for now.

I slowly got up and listened at the door. I could hear Mom talking and the *clink* of a spoon in a bowl, which meant Tanner was slurping his cereal. I didn't want to stay in my room, but I didn't want to go downstairs either. I grabbed my phone. With all of the drama the night before, I had completely forgotten to check it. I looked at the screen, and there were eighteen messages, ranging from **did a big scary monster eat you????** to **OMG she came back and now she's gone again!** from my best friends, Tamiko and Sierra. I sent a couple of quick texts to them, and within seconds my phone was buzzing, as I'd known it would be.

Just then Mom knocked at my door and opened it. "Good morning, sweetie!" she said with her new Sally Sunshine voice that I was already not liking. "I'm so glad to have my girl home!"

I looked at her. Was she just going to pretend nothing had happened?

Mom came in and sat down on my bed. "Dad left for work, but I took this week off. The movers are coming in a couple of days, and we'll need time to settle into our new house." She looked at me. I stared at the wall. The wall of my room, where I had lived since I was a baby. I looked at the spot behind the door, and Mom followed my eyes. She sighed. Since I had been tiny, Dad had measured me on the wall on my birthday and had made a little mark at the top of my head. He'd even done it last year, even though I'd told him I was way too old. "I'm going to miss this house," she said softly. "It has a lot of memories."

It was quiet for a second. Mom looked like she was far away.

"You took your first steps in the kitchen," she said, really smiling this time. "And remember your seventh birthday party that we had in the back-yard?" I did. It was a fairy tea party, and each kid got fairy wings and a magic wand. There had been so many birthdays and holidays in this house.

I had never lived in another house. All I knew was this one. I knew that there were thirty-eight steps between the front porch and the bus stop. I could run up the stairs to the second floor in eight seconds (Tanner and I had timed each other), and I knew that the cabinet door in the kitchen where we kept the cookies creaked when you opened it.

"I think you'll like the new house," said Mom. "Houses. You'll have two homes."

I looked straight ahead.

"Your new room has bookcases all around it. I thought of you when I saw it and knew you would love it." Mom looked at me. "And there's a really great backyard to hang out in. I'm thinking about getting a hammock maybe, and definitely some comfy rocking chairs."

"What about my new other house?" I asked.

"Well," Mom said, "Dad's house is an apartment, actually, and it has really cool views. It's modern, and my house is more old-fashioned. It's the best of both worlds!"

I sighed.

Mom sighed. "Honey, I know this is tough."

I still didn't answer. Mom stood up.

"Well, kiddo, we have a lot to do. I'm guessing

Tamiko and Sierra are coming over soon?"

I looked at my phone lighting up. "Maybe," I said.

Mom nodded. "Okay. Well, let me know what you want to do today. It's your first day back. Tomorrow, though, we do need to pack up your room. Dad and I have been packing things up for the past few weeks, but there's still a lot to do."

I looked into the hall. I must have missed the fact that there were some boxes stacked there. One was marked "Mom" and one was marked "Dad."

Mom followed my gaze. "We're trying to make sure there are familiar things in each house. You can split up your room or . . . I was thinking maybe you'd like to get a new bedroom set?" There was that fake bright happy voice again.

I looked around the room. I liked my room. If the house couldn't stay the same, at least my room could. "No," I said. "I want this stuff."

"We should also talk about your new school," Mom said.

I looked down at my feet. My toenails were painted in my camp colors, blue and yellow. I wiggled them.

"You're already enrolled, but I talked to the principal about having you come over to take a tour and maybe meet some of your new teachers."

I shrugged.

"I think it might be good to take a ride over, just so you are familiar with it before your first day," she said. "It's a bigger school, so you could get the lay of the land. And I've been asking around the new neighborhood, and there are a few girls who will be in your grade."

I nodded.

"Okay," she said brightly. "Well, we have this week to do that, so we'll just find a good time to go."

I swallowed hard.

Mom stood in the doorway and waited a minute, then stepped back into the room quickly, gathered me up in her arms, and hugged me tightly. "It's going to be better, baby girl," she said, kissing the top of my head like she used to when I was little. She was using her normal voice again. "I promise you, it might be hard, but it's definitely going to be better."

I tried really, really hard not to cry. A few tears spilled out, and Mom wiped them away. She took my face in her hands and looked at me. "Now," she said, "first things first, because I think there's a griddle that's calling our names."

I knew the tradition, so I had to smile.

"Welcome-back pancakes!" we said at the same time. Mom's blueberry pancakes were my welcome-home-from-camp tradition. She always put ice cream on them to make them into smiley faces and wrote "XO" in syrup on my plate. I could already taste them. I stood up and followed Mom downstairs. Maybe she was right about things. This day was already getting a little bit better.